The Farrier's Daughter

The Farrier's Daughter

The Irish Witch Series

Leigh Ann Edwards

TULE
PUBLISHING

Dedication

My first novel, The Farrier's Daughter, is dedicated to the two most important and inspirational women in my life.

Thanks to my mum, Joan Edwards who instilled a love of reading and romanticism within me. Her love and pride in me and my writing encouraged me to continue.

And also to Darla, my only sister and very best friend...her unending support, as well as her belief that it is never too late to pursue your passion, were a great inspiration to me.

Although neither are here to see me realize my dream of having my novels published, I can still feel their love and support, and I know they continue to cheer me on for they truly were my biggest fans!

ACKNOWLEDGMENTS

I would like to thank Danielle Rayner, editorial assistant and my first contact at Tule Publishing. Thank you so much for falling in love with The Irish Witch Series, for believing in my writing, and for being instrumental in seeing that my novels were published by Tule. I truly appreciate all your help and for going to bat for me.

Thanks to Meghan Farrell for your vast knowledge and expertise in contractual and editorial matters, and for making my experience with Tule so positive. I am very grateful for your assistance.

Thank you to Lindsey Stover editorial and marketing manager at Tule. I'm so pleased with all the great promotional strategies you are working on to ensure my novel is properly marketed and widely visible to readers.

Thanks to the editorial staff for all your great recommendations and support.

I'd also like to acknowledge and thank Ravven for the absolutely amazing and appealing book covers she designed for my series.

Thank you to my husband Mark who shares my love of history and traveling, who inspires me by taking me to the UK and Ireland, and who definitely understands how much my writing means to me.

To my beautiful daughters, Katrina and Jerilyn who

while growing up possibly felt they needed to compete with my writing...thanks for realizing that writing is my passion, but that both of you are my heart.

Thanks to my precious grandchildren, Darien, Daniella, Grayson and Novak who are a constant source of joy and inspiration.

Thank-you to my brother, Kerry, although he claims reading a "love scene" scarred him for life, he has been very supportive and his humour is a gift that has lightened my troubles so often through the years.

Thanks also to my sister-in-law, Tannis who has always been so confident in my abilities as a writer. She's been very patient in waiting for so long for me to get my books published so I can continue writing, and she can "finally" learn the ending.

As mentioned in the dedication page, thanks to Mum and my sister, Darla for always believing in me and nurturing my dream.

I would like to thank my many friends through the years who have supported my writing and offered much encouragement.

Each and every one of you has contributed to ensuring "The Farrier's Daughter" became more than just a manuscript in a binder!

Chapter One

THE TWO WOMEN stood talking outside the bedchamber, trying to keep their concerned whispers from the boy inside. A small child sat at their feet, staring intently at a butterfly on the nearby windowsill. "Will he live through this, Morag?" asked one of the women. "It has been near a month since his ordeal. I thought he would heal faster, as he was always such a strong boy."

"Aye, he's strong, Milady, or he'd not have survived those dreadful wounds. And, he made it through the fever and the festering when I thought he wouldn't. In truth, his wounds have all but healed. Sure, 'tis his soul that's sorely damage. I fear he has lost all will, Milady, and all hope." The butterfly helplessly fluttered about attempting to take flight, but to no avail. Noticing its broken wing, the child stood and walked determinedly toward the arched window.

"Aye, I've thought so myself, Morag. My heart breaks for him. He is only ten and two. His mother and sister passed on from the fever, not six months ago. Then, his father's castle was scourged. He apparently watched his father and brother slain before him, and the vicious marauders left the child for dead. My husband and his army found him there on the battlefield, hidden amongst the dead bodies. I cannot imagine the horror of it!"

Morag pressed a handkerchief to her eyes.

The child glanced at the women noting their deep empathy and the older woman's uncommon display of emotion. With a new urgency she carefully picked up the butterfly and tenderly placed it on her open palm. Assessing the damaged wing she softly traced the broken wing with her tiny finger, and then gently blew upon it. Almost immediately she watched it spread both wings and capably soar skyward. A satisfied smile crossed her small face.

"He is my husband's nephew, Morag, so he has always been dear to me, and his mother was also my dearest childhood friend. What can I do to save her child in her stead? He will barely speak to me, save an aye or nay when I ask him something directly."

"I believe most importantly, he must start to eat more heartily. If he doesn't take nourishment soon, he will not regain his strength and he may very well die."

"I have tried, Morag, truly I have."

"I do not fault you, Milady. If his spirit is broken, and his heart is breakin' as well, there's little to be done to convince him fillin' his stomach is necessary. Have ye tried gettin' yer sons to talk with him? They're his age, are they not?" The child returned to her position near the two women, once more intent on listening to them, her pointy chin lifted in concentration. "Aye, my twins are but a year younger than him, and they were always such good friends. Now, he barely seems to acknowledge them. We thought to take him outside just the other day, as you'd suggested, but he'd have no part of it. He simply wants to lie in that bed."

"I fear he's made up his mind. He'll go to the beyond with his kin, then, Milady?"

"Oh no, Morag, we must prevent that by whatever measures need be taken!" The small child slipped past them and into the room with the ailing boy.

⌘

SENSING A PRESENCE, he opened his eyes. A child's face hovered inches away. Bright blue eyes met his, and long golden hair seemed to surround him. He frowned and closed his eyes, again, presuming she would leave, but a breath tickled his nose and his lids opened of their own accord. She stood there still, staring down at him. Irritated, he huffed and turned over to face the opposite wall. The small footsteps receded and he thought she'd left him at last, but, when he dared a peek, he saw her peering curiously from the other side of the bed. Uttering a disapproving snarl, he turned over, once more.

"Have they cut out your tongue, then?"

Startled, he jumped as he lay, and glared. "No, they've not cut out my tongue. I can speak well enough. But, why would I desire to speak with the likes of you?" When she remained standing there, silently gazing at him, he snapped, "Why are you here?"

"I've come to look at you."

"Aye, well, sure you've done that, then, so you can leave."

"I don't wish to leave, as yet."

"Aye, but I do. I demand you leave this room this very minute!"

"Make me!" she challenged.

"Would you have me beat you, you wee pest?"

"You haven't the strength," she taunted.

Throwing aside the bed covers, he jerked upright, only to fall back on the pillows as his head spun. "Are you addle-minded, girl?" he growled.

"I am kin to your chieftain. You should not provoke me! I could have you thrown in the dungeon!"

"They do not throw children in the dungeon in this castle. Our chieftain is a fair and just man, and why would he throw me in the dungeon? What wrong have I done?"

"You've disturbed my rest."

"You've rested long enough," she said, attempting to plump his pillows. He refused the gesture by stiffly pulling away from her. She was not to be dissuaded and she plunked herself upon his bed. "Why not play a game with me, boy?"

"I am not a boy, I'm a man—" the girl coughed "—or nearly, at any rate. And do you think I look as though I want to play games with a stupid girl-child?"

Her blue eyes narrowed slightly and she lifted her chin. "Are you fearful of losing to a girl-child?"

"I could win any game against you!" he snapped, his nostrils flaring in displeasure. "You're hardly more than a baby. What is your age?"

"I am five years your younger."

"And why should I want to play a game with the farrier's daughter who is but seven years old?"

"And how is it you know who I am?" she demanded, placing her hands on her hips.

"I've seen you about with my cousins, a time or two."

"But, why did you remember me?"

"I remember your pretty, er, long golden hair." He blushed, then, spit out, "And you have strange eyes, an odd shade of blue."

"I remember you as well, Killian O'Brien. You were once fleet of foot and as swift and skilled as your cousins at longbow, skean, and sword."

"I am stronger and more skillful than either Rory or Riley."

"They train constantly and grow more capable each day while you choose to lie in this bed. Sure, they have surpassed your abilities by now."

"Why would that concern me?" he snarled.

"I thought it was important to all O'Briens to remain strong and courageous and unfaltering."

He leaned toward her, his face red with anger. "It is important to me, as well!"

"But you have faltered," she whispered. His eyes blazed and she hurriedly hopped off the bed, capably dancing out of his range and away from his fury.

"You have no right to condemn me!" His bottom lip trembled slightly. "You know nothing of what has happened to me and mine!"

"I know some."

"Aye, well, don't you think anyone might falter if they'd suffered this?" He pulled open his nightshirt to reveal a long purple gash that ran from nape to navel. The welted scar was raised and angry, but no angrier than the boy who possessed it. Tears brimmed in his eyes and he fought valiantly to stem them.

" 'Tis a proud battle's scar you possess, Killian O'Brien," she murmured. He sat up higher at her praise. "But you've lived through the battle and now you must live on past the battle, for that is what warriors do. Are you not to be a chieftain, one day?"

His pain-filled eyes met hers. "I thought I would, but I no longer see the glory in it. My body has healed, but I fear my heart never will."

"It will take longer," she soothed. "Wounds of the heart always do." He found himself relaxing and he now allowed her to prop the pillows behind him so he sat upright. Neither child heard the women approaching the door.

⌘

"OH MILADY, SHE'S in there with the lad," Morag said, an eye pressed to the crack of the door. "She doesn't usually disobey me so. She knows she's not to interfere in my healing! She'll be chattin' his ear off, there's little doubt of that."

"But Morag, listen," the chieftain's wife urged. "He is responding to her."

"Aye, he's probably complainin' about the incessant chatter for she's a wee gabber, she is! But no matter, if her rilin' him has spurred him to speak, so be it."

"Praise be spoken to the gods for sending the dear child if she is able to help him."

"Aye, then best we leave her with him awhile longer," Morag whispered, softly shutting the door.

⌘

"SO, KILLIAN O'BRIEN, will you play the game with me?" asked the girl, settling on his bed, once more.

"What type of game is it? A game for girls to play?" he sniffed.

"No, 'tis a game anyone can play. 'Tis one I created. There are few rules so it will be easy enough for you to learn." He scowled at this. "But if you win this game, in truth, you lose, for it is called My Plight is Greater."

"Sounds dim-witted to me. When I play a game, I like to win, and, given my circumstances, it is unlikely your plight could be as great as mine."

"Do not be so certain," she said, lifting an eyebrow.

"How, then, do you begin?" he demanded. "Who starts?"

"You may, if you like."

"No, since 'tis your game, you begin. But what is your name, girl, or should I simply refer to you as the farrier's daughter?"

"It is Alainn."

His green eyes caught hers and he blushed again. "That is an unusual name."

"Aye, it is Gaelic for lovely. My mother named me, but I cannot recall anything about her, so that is how I shall begin." She clasped her hands on her lap. "My mother died when I was only months old."

"Aye, well, I lost my mother just months ago, so my grief is still fresh." His eyebrows contracted at the memory of it.

"But my plight is greater," she went on candidly, "as I did not know a mother's love, and I do not even have memories of her to console me."

"Aye, but it hurt me all the more to have had her and to have lost her!"

"But you had her love, her nurturing and affection for a dozen years."

He rarely allowed himself to think about his mother for it was still too painful, but this small girl had never even known her own mother, so he decided she presented an arguable point. "I've lost a sister, and now my brother, too, only recently."

"But you had a brother and sister to play with and confide in, to tell secrets to and to grow with. My parents were very old when I came to be. I have heard it said it was a miracle that I was born at all, as my mother was a half-century and seven at the time of my birth and my father a decade older. So, I never knew what it was to have a sibling or to be a sister."

"But, how can you miss what you never had?" he asked, leaning forward.

Her determined face was only inches from his own. "I know what I have missed out on."

He contemplated this and thought, perhaps, she was correct, for he would always treasure his time with his brother and sister no matter how much his heart ached with the loneliness of losing them. He sat up straighter and took his turn at the game. "My father is gone now, as well, and your father still lives, so there is no disputing my plight is greater."

"Aye, my father lives, he is old and ailing, but he still lives, and just outside the castle walls, but I do not live with him. My father turned me out when I was but three years of age."

The boy hadn't known this about the child. "He turned you out? Where do you live, then?"

"He sent me to live with Morag."

"You live with Morag the Wise Woman!" he blurted. "You've clearly won this round, for your plight is truly greater! She may be a noted healer, but she is a wretched old crone. She is wicked and miserable, and her potions are bitter! My father used to say she was older than dirt, even back when he was a child." She giggled and he smiled back, liking the sound of her laugh. The smile felt foreign on his face.

"She is not as prickly as she appears. 'Tis true she is strict and has strong opinions and expectations, but I owe her much."

Killian thought her a loyal sort to defend the old woman. He knit his brows and asked, "But why would he have you live with Morag?"

"She has raised other girls."

"But, why would he turn you out? Did he think he could not raise a girl-child on his own?"

"Perhaps, that is part of it, but mostly," she said, dropping her gaze and picking at the bed covers, "it is because he fears me."

He snorted. "He fears you? Why ever would he fear a small girl like you, and his own daughter?"

She snapped her eyes back up and whispered, "Because, I know of magic."

Killian smirked. "Of course you know of magic, everyone knows of magic. We live in Ireland. Everyone knows of fairies and druids, and the like. Magic cannot be disputed, even if the priests do not take kindly to these beliefs."

"Aye, but I can do magic."

Chapter Two

H IS EYES WIDENED. "You're tellin' me you're a fairy?"

"No, fairies have never been human. Morag says when a human possesses magical abilities they are witches. I am a witch."

"I might have you burned at the stake, then, if you're truly a witch."

She giggled behind her hands. "Witches may be suspect in Ireland, but they are not burned."

"True enough, they're not burned as in France or Scotland, but they have been known to be banished from the castle walls," he cautioned, "and made to live in shame and squalor."

"Ah, you speak of the Glade Witch. Well, I suppose your grandfather had no choice but to banish her. She did put a curse on him and his line."

"And it's still not ended."

She shook her head soberly. "I speak to her sometimes."

"You do not!"

"Aye, but I do!"

"How would you get to her cave? You are a small child

and it is a goodly walk through the stone close and around the fairy glade, it is."

"I don't go around the fairy glade."

He gasped. "You can't mean you go through it? We are forbidden to go into the fairies' realm. They would snatch you up!" He crossed his arms and sat back against his pillows. "You must be lying."

"I do not tell lies," she said firmly, setting her chin. "And, why would you believe I am a witch but not that I have been in the fairy glade?"

"I did not say I believe you. What powers do you claim to have?"

"Well, there're the colors. People claim I am a good judge of character, but it is because I see the colored glow around people."

"What nonsense is that?" he scoffed.

"No, 'tis not nonsense," she insisted. "Morag knows of it, though she says I should not speak of it. She says magic must be left to the fairies and that no good comes of people possessing magical powers. But, she calls the colors auras. 'Tis a hazy glow that encircles each person, reflecting what is in the soul."

"Like a halo, then?" He found himself nearly believing.

"Aye, some are like a halo about the head, but some are a glow about the entire body. And, the glow can change in color and strength depending on happenings in the person's life, good and bad."

"Then, mine must be black as pitch."

"Some people have black souls. Thick, dark, muddy clouds that hover about them. They frighten me, the dark ones. But, yours is not dark, Killian O'Brien. Yours is as green as your eyes, and as vibrant as the rolling hills past our River Shannon. It has faded some with your misfortune, but it will brighten." He pursed his lips slightly, showing his skepticism. "You cannot always tell what color the glow will be," she said patiently, "for it is not always what you believe it should be. Your uncle's priest has a dark gray cloud around him and the Glade Witch's son has a lovely, sunny yellow glow. It brightens when I play with him."

"You play with her malformed son? Is he truly as grotesque as I have heard?"

Frowning down her nose, she sniffed. "He is not grotesque. Sure, he isn't the same as most, for he has a misshapen face. His mouth and teeth are not entirely as they should be. He walks with a limp for one foot is turned inward, and he has a large bump upon his back."

"He sounds quite hideous to me."

"But he has a kind heart and gentle eyes." Her face softened. "It saddens me that everyone speaks cruel of him. He can do nothing about his maladies and no one can choose who they are born to."

"If you are truly a witch, what other powers do you possess aside from seeing colors?" he asked, curious, and wanting to lighten her mood.

"Morag says I am a seer. I know what is to happen at times. And, I am a healer. I use the herbs and potions as Morag does, but I am a natural healer, as well. I heal with my hands. And, sometimes, I can move things, but only if I am very angry or dreadfully fearful."

"You can move things? Explain this!"

"With my mind, I can look at something and make it move. That disturbed my father greatly."

"Is that what drove him to drink?" He spoke the words without thinking. Everyone in the castle knew of the farrier's affliction with drink, but he doubted his young daughter had knowledge of that.

"No, he drank well enough even back in the days when I lived with him," she said, startling him with her knowledge and candor. "He came home, one night, his mind affected by too much drink, stumblin' into the cottage. I feared he might fall and crack his head or break his neck, and I caused the embers in the fire to roar and blaze without going near the hearth. When he nearly fell down in dismay, I sent a chair across the room to catch his fall so that he'd not hit the floor, but he did so anyway."

"You're not lyin', are you?"

"No, I have told you. Sure, I do not utter lies." Her eyes grew wider and she pointed her tiny finger at him.

"And, is that the extent of your witchcraft, then?" he mocked, displeased by how intrigued he was with the child.

She glanced toward the door and leaned close to whisper

in his ear, "Morag says I must not mention this, for there is great suspicion about people who can see spirits of those who have passed on."

"You see spirits?" His face paled. "All spirits?"

"No, I have no control over what spirits I see. They mostly come to me if they need to talk before they go to the beyond."

"Do you see my mother?"

"No. Your sister tells me she has gone on."

He jolted back with the fear of it, then, flushed an angry red. "Now, I know you are lying! You're nothin' but a spinner of tales!" he accused. "You told me you do not tell lies."

"I am not lying."

"My mother would not leave my sister behind. She was her youngest child. Her sweet baby."

"But she died before your sister. Your sister did not fall ill until the evening after your mother passed."

His face, already a milky pallor, drained its color entirely when he realized she knew these truths. "How could you know that? Have you truly spoken with Nola?"

"Aye, she sits beside you on your bed this very moment." Tears pooled in his deep green eyes, once more, and he suddenly looked small and lost. "She was deeply attached to you in life. She will not go on as she fears for your life and wants you to become well."

"Perhaps, she waits for me to join her?" he asked softly.

"Then, why would she ask me to heal you?"

"She will not go on to heaven to join our parents and my brother until I am healed?" She bit her lip and shook her head. "Then heal me!" he demanded. "And, come to it, why haven't you healed me before this?"

"You wouldn't have believed in my healing or accepted it, for you had no desire to live! Morag doesn't allow me to practice magic openly for she believes people will misunderstand and think I am evil. And I must lay my hand to the wounds to truly heal them, though I did charm the salves and ointments she put on your wounds, and the elixirs you drank."

"Well, she is not here at the moment," he said, shifting on the bed. "So, heal me further. Heal my wounds and my heart and make me stronger, as well." Her eyes met his and he no longer thought of the unusual shade of blue as strange, but simply enchanting. She smiled warmly and placed her small hand on his brutal scar.

Warmth radiated from her hand, seeming to sear right through him. They stared as the dark purple wound faded to light pink. She lifted her hand and moved away from him. "But what of the scar?" he asked. "Can't you make it go away entirely? And, I am still weak and grieving."

"You demand much, Killian O'Brien," she chastised. "Those tasks are not within my power. Though your strength may be greatly improved, you must work on that yourself. Your heart must heal in its own time, as well, for if you do not grieve for those you have lost, you will never be free of the pain that you feel."

"Will Nola leave, now that I am on the path to healing?"

"Aye, she's gone." His loneliness and gloom spread palpably through the room. She looked into his sad eyes. "Did you actually witness your father's death, Killian O'Brien?"

"No." He hesitated. "I saw him wounded, watched the barbarians drag him away."

"Why would they take him away and not end his life there on the battlefield as they had so many others?"

His face crumpled in despair, but he seemed compelled to answer her. "I cannot say. Perhaps, they wanted to torture him since he was an important chieftain of my mother's family, the O'Donnels. They are in alliance with clan O'Neill who has many enemies."

"Maybe, he was only taken prisoner," she suggested, "to use for bargaining with the O'Neills or with your uncle." He considered this for a moment, and the color returned to his face.

"Could he be alive? Can you see it with your powers? Are you able?" he asked, hope shining in his eyes.

"I cannot always see things, especially if I dare to conjure a vision. But, I can try. I need water or sand or the like if I am to attempt it."

"The water basin, there, on the stand. Fetch it," he commanded, taking charge. "Bring it here to the bed." She narrowed her eyes at his harsh manner, and he hastily added,

"Please."

She carried the basin across the room, struggling under the heavy load, and he had to remind himself she was just a small child no matter what powers she seemed to possess. She went back for the pitcher while he watched.

"If you can move articles why do you not employ your powers to assist you in chores of this nature?"

"It is as I have said, I must be filled with deep emotion to attempt such feats, and Morag says the more I use my abilities the more powerful my magic will become. She fears I will one day be unable to control it, so I must abide her wisdom." When she finally managed to get the pitcher to him, he helped her pour the water.

"Now, what do you do?"

She glared impatiently but explained, "I must concentrate extremely intently on your father, though I can only scarcely recall his face from when he was once at this castle. You may be able to help me with it. Here, take my hand and think as hard as you can on summoning your father's face into your mind's eye. And, be as quiet as you can."

He took her hand and noticed how truly small it was. He barely dared to let himself breathe for fear it would disturb her concentration and stared at the water for what felt like an eternity. Nothing seemed to be happening. When he was about to give up, he noticed tiny ripples starting to form in the water. She let out a tiny gasp and he could remain silent no longer. "What do you see?"

"He is not dead. I see him. I cannot say where. Only, that he lives." With that, she hopped off the bed, nearly spilling the basin as she rushed it across the room.

"Where are you going?" he called, not wanting her to leave.

"Morag approaches and she is sure to be angered at my disobedience." She busied herself replacing the basin and pitcher. "I must also tell your cousins that tomorrow you will be out sparring with them. They shall be greatly relieved, for they've fretted much about your state. You are important to them. And, I will tell your aunt to bring you a tray of food, for Morag says you must eat."

"Girl!" he called after her.

When she turned, he saw the displeased frown on her face. " 'Tis not my name!"

"Lainna," he said.

" 'Tis not my name, either," she pouted, then, angled her eyes, considering it. "But, I like it well enough. You may call me Lainna, Killian O'Brien, for I've a fondness for the manner in which you speak it."

"Lainna," he repeated, enjoying the feel of her name as he spoke it. "What is it I can do to repay you for your deeds?" He watched a sweet smile spread across her rosy lips, and in those unforgettably magical blue eyes, he caught a mischievous sparkle he'd not noticed before.

"I will think of something, Killian O'Brien. One day, I am certain, I will think of a way."

⌘

HE WONDERED WHEN and how the witch-child would call his payment due.

Chapter Three

THE SUN WARMED her back as Alainn tended the aromatic plants of the herb garden. A gentle breeze blew wisps of golden hair against the soft pink of her cheeks, and she breathed in the fragrant perfumes, exhaling with a contented sigh. She adored being in the garden and was possessive toward it. It felt like her garden, though it belonged to the O'Briens as did everything on this land. But, now that Morag was in failing health, it was she who diligently cared for the herbs and flowers, and they flourished under her hand.

A cat crept into the garden, lifting its feet carefully as it minced through the greenery. It was sleek and trim with a shiny black coat. She paused a moment to watch it, then resumed her gardening.

Alainn took pride in her knowledge of herbs. She knew each one, not only by name and form, but smell, even the ones that were supposedly odorless. She knew what quantity and combinations would benefit an ailment and what would impede the healing, what dosage would remedy and how to strengthen it to a poison.

The cat pounced at an imaginary prey, the flowers rustling in protest.

She had learned herbs must be collected in a variety of ways and at different times of day or night. Some needed great caution for if they touched bare skin, they could poison you or effect horrid hallucinations. There were herbs that could drive you to madness, just by touching them. Alainn also knew what herbs healed, but in potions of witchcraft.

Some of this she had learned from Morag in working, studying, and living with her through the many years. Some she had learned from the fairies. Others, she just knew in her mind and felt in her fingers. When the herbal combination was correct, her hand would grow warm. If the quantity was too great or the mixture dangerous, her hand would begin to burn.

The cat slid through the flowers and rubbed her leg as it passed. "Hello, you lovely black cat, how could you possibly bring ill luck?" she crooned, scratching it behind the ears. It pressed into her hand.

Morag was not always in favor of her experiments and would never have thought of, nor attempted, many of the combinations Alainn tried. But, she had been forced to admit the girl had come up with cures or benefits for a variety of conditions.

The cat stretched out next to her and began to purr.

A room adjoining the kitchen was where the two women

dried, cured, mixed, and stored their potions. A great cupboard dominated the room, its shelves lined with bottles of various sizes. Drying herbs, tied with string, hung from the rafters. Baskets and sacks of ingredients sat under a table off to one side. Vessels, mixing tools, and many mortars and pestles, sat on top of it. Morag had been an able alchemist for many years, and Alainn had learned well. They both possessed an exact expertise with a mortar and pestle, as all alchemists needed.

Each herb was stored in a container in the great cupboard, and Alainn knew by heart where each one was kept. She had arranged the system herself and categorized them not only alphabetically, but also by their purpose and potency. There were the extreme poisons and hallucinogenic herbs, such as evening nightshade, cowbane, henbane, mandrake, and monkshood, kept in a separate cupboard within, secured with a padlock. The mild poisons were on the top shelves but always kept in small quantities.

There were select potions used in the treatment of fractures, wounds, and burns. There were the heal-alls, the most important herbs of any garden. And, of course, the magical herbs that Morag allowed Alainn to keep in the cupboard but would not use herself. Morag could not read, so the system was of little purpose to her, but she had appeased Alainn by allowing her to modify it, and, in truth, she believed the girl's way of doing things was probably an improvement.

Beyond the room was a small chamber where people came to seek their assistance. It had a back entrance through a narrow alleyway. There were locks on both the back door and the door that led to the kitchen, and Morag and Alainn were the only people with keys to open them. This allowed the patrons to come in secret if their conditions were of a private and delicate nature.

With the responsibility of being a healer or wise woman, as they were often called, came a vast quantity of knowledge about the nobles who lived in the castle, the staff who served them, and the peasants in the village. All knowledge was confidential and much of it, secretive. The women were privy to which men wanted to enhance their virility, what woman wanted to prevent a pregnancy, and who needed herbs to increase fertility. Some women came for aid in increasing or decreasing their husbands' libidos. An even greater number of men came for a cure for "frigidity," as they referred to it. Only Morag and Alainn knew that the priest was in need of a potion to decrease his carnal urges.

Often, Alainn felt it difficult not to judge their patrons. When women came wanting to end a pregnancy, she always tried to assess the situation. Sometimes, she would under-stand the reasoning. Other times, she could not. It was only Morag who would issue the herbal concoctions for these unwanted pregnancies, for Alainn felt it was not up to her to decide what child should be allowed to be born. Morag reasoned that if a man had been at her and she carried his unwanted child, it was better than flinging herself from the nearby cliff, as women had oft been known to do.

There were the men who came to the healers for remedies for diseases contracted through bedding unclean women in brothels. Alainn thought it would be fitting to have their minds and bodies rot for their indiscretions, but then she would think of their wives and feel greatly for their plight. In truth, the ointments and liniments would only treat the symptoms and give temporary relief, for there was no cure known to Alainn for that manner of disease. And, abstinence from such activities was the only prevention, though she was never allowed to give her opinion on that.

Alainn was also astute in learning how to prepare concoctions that added to wellness and cleanliness of their patrons. She had swayed many a person to her way of thinking regarding washing regularly and even bathing, when it was possible. Many people still washed only in cold water, and only their hands and faces, for they believed the warm water would invite evil into their bodies. Alainn tended to disagree and convinced many that the more you washed the less apt you would be to become ill or diseased, and she reasoned being clean was good for the soul.

Many women were most appreciative of the cures Alainn had prepared for pain associated with their monthlies, and in childbed, as well. Her fragrant concoctions and additives to oils and soaps, for skin and hair, and unconventional body cleansers were much sought after by women. Alainn had discovered a pinch of this and a dash of that seemed to make the hair shine radiantly. Certain herbs and oils made the scent of soaps much more pleasant and less harsh on the skin. Mint, when added to the balm and grit mixture for cleaning teeth, made it much more pleasing to the taste.

Lady Siobhan was most grateful, praising Alainn often, as she came to select from the creams and balms the young woman had prepared. The chieftain's priest was clearly not in favor of applying anything to the body for he believed it was a sin for a person to touch their bodies in any area other than their hands and face.

Alainn, against Morag's better judgment, was also helpful in procuring potions of love for maidens in want of a husband or lover, though she drew the line if the man was already married or if a mistress asked for aid in such matters. She took pride in the knowledge they helped many through times of illness and injury, and loneliness and fearfulness, for many herbs offered a cure for nervousness or melancholy.

She sighed and petted the soft fur, now warm under the sun, when the sound of the chieftain's sons battling with broadswords broke into her thoughts. The clashes were loud and rapid and she turned to watch them spar. She listened as the two swords clanged out loudly, then the twins' laughter erupted as she saw one sword fall to the ground. A dove emitted its distinctive call, a crow cawed loudly in response and she heard the chieftain's nephew speaking to her, continuing on with their present conversation.

"Alainn, we have had this discussion many times previous. Learning the way of the sword should truly be left to menfolk!"

She turned up her nose, rolled her eyes, and feigned agreement.

"Oh, aye, and women should contentedly cook and clean and bear children since we are weaker and dafter and only capable of menial tasks or childbirth?" she sarcastically quipped.

Her face darkened and she glanced sharply toward the north solar. The chieftain stood at the window of his private chamber in the castle tower, eyes fixed on her. She squeezed the cat reflexively and it ran off with a hiss. Alainn had not intended to hear the chieftain's thoughts, but they had come to her, nonetheless.

She was accustomed to men looking at her, and, though she'd never been with a man in such a manner, she was aware of the powerful force of men's desires. On more than one occasion, she had used the dagger she kept hidden in her apron pocket to ward off their carnal intentions. She found it odd, the number of ways men could look at her and the variety of her reactions. There were those who looked at her and she felt pleased at the attention, as though they were just showing appreciation of a woman's form. But, others ogled her in such a lewd manner, she felt them stripping off her garments with their eyes, making her skin crawl, making her fearful of meeting them alone.

She was embarrassed to admit that she was flattered the chieftain would take notice of her, but she found herself uncomfortable in the knowledge that if he decided to take her to his bed, she would be expected to partake without question or dispute. Alainn patted the weapon within her pocket as if to reassure herself it would be there the next time it was needed, though, to use it against the chieftain would be treasonous and punishable by hanging. It would not be an option, and she prayed it would never come to that. Perhaps his interest was merely a passing thought and nothing more.

Alainn had always trusted Hugh O'Brien, defended him as a chieftain and as a man, but recently she had sensed a profound change in him. Although always a strong and demanding ruler, of late, she felt herself questioning the man's integrity. His moods were often dark and his temper, unreasonably short.

She looked toward the north solar once more, closed her senses to all that was transpiring around her, and focused her mind on the chieftain's thoughts, willing her mind to merge with the O'Brien. As though a bird in flight, her mind soared up and up, and the world tilted dizzyingly. She opened her eyes and found herself looking down upon the countryside, seeing through the chieftain's eyes. Not simply hearing his thoughts but thinking them. She willed him to reflect upon the last decade.

Chapter Four

H UGH O'BRIEN FELT an entirely odd sensation as he
stood in his tower bedchamber. One moment, he had
been thinking about the farrier's young daughter and, the
next, he found himself adrift in memories of the past, to the
time when he had lost his younger brother, Kieran, when his
son had come to live with him and the old healer and young
girl had mended him.

He had seen his younger brother avenged. All of the clan
McCarthy who had been responsible for the attack on his
brother's castle had been killed or scattered across the
country. They had not been heard from for some time.

His younger brother, Kieran, had never been found,
though his son, Killian, insisted he may yet live. With his
army, Hugh had scoured the countryside, searching every
pitiful dungeon, but no trace of his fondest brother had been
discovered. He had been loath to give up the search, but
recalled the day he had deemed it necessary.

The captain of the guard, a strongly built Scot on his
immense brown steed, headed toward the chieftain clearly
uncertain how to broach the subject of ending the lengthy

search. He cleared his throat as he approached the O'Brien.

"A word, Milord," the uniformed man stammered.

"Aye, Captain!"

The man obviously searched for the correct words, his eyes filled with a hint of dread.

"Go on, Mac, yer not one to beat about the bush; say what's on your mind!"

"Aye, Milord, to be certain. Well … it has been months now, and we are no closer to learnin' the truth, we've had no leads for quite some time! The men are tired and frankly, Milord, they're losin' hope. Still, ye ken they'll follow ye without question should you care to continue."

Hugh O'Brien looked around him. He studied each man as they sat atop their horses. It was true, the men were exhausted. He was exhausted! He felt the ache within his bones. Disheartened, he inhaled the damp air. "Aye, I know it well enough, Mac, they're a loyal lot, but 'tis true, sure we can't keep searchin' for my brother forever with no hope to go on."

Sighing deeply once more he glanced at the other man. "Tell the men we head home this day."

Hugh had finally resigned himself to his brother's death, from wounds inflicted during the pillage or as punishment, thereafter. However, Keiran's son, now a man, had never accepted it.

The following decade had been mostly peaceful. The chieftain's tenants and servants remained loyal, as did the surrounding clans who had formed an alliance several years previous. Hugh O'Brien thought himself fortunate indeed to have known this time of peace. There were many clans still at battle with each other and in conflict amongst themselves. Their allegiances were so varied and volatile it was a feat to keep abreast of who sided with what clan, and they could change in a heartbeat. He knew of brothers murdering brothers to gain control of the chieftainship, daughters who plotted against fathers to ensure their sons would become earls or lords. He'd heard of slaying by poison and sword, of abductions of men and women, alike. It seemed murder and mayhem reigned throughout much of the country. He was grateful his brothers trusted in his leadership and seemed disinclined to overthrow him.

With a nod, he silently thanked the Normans who built the grand castle in which he lived. It had proved impenetrable, thus far. Strategically placed on the banks of the River Shannon and accessible only by drawbridge, it was a strong fortress. The walled village beyond the castle gates had remained mostly unmarred, as well. His alliance with the O'Neills and his wife's family, the O'Rorkes, surely dissuaded enemy clans from beginning a feud that could not be won.

Even the running of his earldom was smooth and orderly. There were the usual offenses and misdeeds found in any village and castle, and his dungeon was not always empty, to be certain, but he employed a champion steward, an apt levier of taxes, and a knowledgeable captain. Hugh O'Brien considered himself a contented man for the most part.

He was not certain how long this peace would last throughout his land, for, at the meeting of the Council of the Clans, it was reported the younger Henry, King Henry VIII of England who had taken power some years before, was building an army to overthrow the Irish or anyone who resisted him. There were rumblings of the English enforcing their rule on the chieftain, once more, and, to the east, minor battles had already been fought.

Centuries before, the Irish had been great kings and noblemen, but the English had invaded and taken over. They had stripped the chieftains of their kingship and, though they kept the noble title of earl or lord, the English had inflicted much pain and terror on the Irish, as in so many lands. In the Kildare Proclamation, they had ordered that Irish language, dress, and customs be forfeited and replaced with those of the English, with penalty of death for donning an Irish garment or using a Gaelic phrase. And, though the chieftains had regained much of their control in the last century and many of their customs and language had been regained, Ireland would never be considered pure Irish again. At one time, Hugh believed he would never willingly side with the English and, in his heart, he hoped it would never come to that. He'd always believed he would rather die fighting for the cause of his people than be ruled by the arrogant English.

The Council of the Clans was much divided on what must be done, as were many of the clans themselves. Even men within each clan. Many planned to fight to the death for their right of all things Irish, but others thought the cost may be too great. They had already decided not to enter a war that could not be won, as the English army was both massive and skilled. Their empire was the wealthiest in the world. Their weaponry, much advanced and seemingly endless.

Hugh O'Brien thought greatly about the enormous decision that must be made, and sooner than he would like. Would his clan choose to bend to the ways of the English to ensure no more Irish people died at their hands, or would living under their rule be too great a burden to bear? Often, when a chieftain, or earl, as the English would have them known, sided with them, he was able to retain authority of his people and, though the rents the English demanded were often high and their laws, rigid and unfair, their scrutiny was much less strict than with clans who opposed them. The English still had power to the east in the pale in Dublin, but they had become much less effective where the clans and chieftains flourished.

Hugh had always been of the mindset that the clans would have been wise, decades previous, to end their infamous feuding and battling, and rally their forces. For, if they were weakened by civil battles, then, who among them would remain to ward off the detestable English if they came to conquer in the name of the Tudor king? He had said his piece many times at council, but it seemed to fall on deaf ears, for, though powerful men, they oft acted as raucous children who could not be reasoned with. Century old feuding was difficult to end by suggestion.

Such dismal thoughts always left him weary of body and soul, and the bitter elixir he procured from the alchemist in the city was not proving effective. He felt no younger, no less tired, and, in truth, he did not feel entirely himself these days. His temper was harsh. His thoughts often cloudy. Perhaps it was time to hand over the reins to one of his sons. They would soon be ready. The grand celebrations of their milestone birthday were less than three moons away. Either of them would be a most capable leader, with some advice and assistance from himself and his brothers. Hugh was undeniably proud of his two strong, skillful lads. Aye, they would do him favor when the time came for a new chieftain.

He was most fortunate his sons had been born before that damnable witch had cursed his line. Perhaps, he was more inclined to side with the English than some because clan O'Brien was threatened by the curse, and its sheer existence was in jeopardy.

His father would never tell him exactly what had transpired between him and the woman, but he knew the outcome. She'd inflicted blight upon his brothers and himself. If their wives did not mysteriously become barren, they bore stillborn children, or children who lived but hours.

He and his dear wife had lost five babes and he knew how her arms ached to hold another child. He knew how she longed to have a daughter.

And now, his own wife would no longer share his bed for fear of becoming with child. He clearly remembered when she'd confessed she could not bear to lose another child.

"But, you are my wife, and I love and desire you as much as the day we were wed, Siobhan. How can you deny me? Physical love is meant to be shared between a man and a woman. If you love me as you claim to…"

"Hugh, this has naught to do with love or desire, for I shall never fail you on those counts! But if you love me as you claim, you will not ask me to risk my heart being shattered by the loss of yet another child! I could not bear it! We both know I would never recover! Some days, even now, I think I should like to lie in the ground with all my lost wee babes! All taken because of a witch's curse! No, Hugh, I shall never again share your bed, not while I am of an age to bear children. So seek the company of others if you must, or wait if you can. Though I shall not ask you to remain true to your marriage vow for my mind is set on this, unless you take me by force, we shall not be joined in intimacy, not for a goodly while!"

For this, he hated the witch most of all. His desire for his wife was still great, and now there was a wedge between them that made being alone together most awkward.

Two of his brothers' wives had never produced children,

and another had lost more infants than he and his wife. His youngest brother, Sean, had been blessed with a son, now ten years old, but had lost his wife in the process as she had died after giving birth. Of the six brothers O'Brien, there were only four lads to carry on the name. Even his brother, Kieran, who had left to rule as chieftain of his wife's clan, had been affected by the unholy hex. His castle was a hard day's ride from here, but the curse had reached even there. He was fortunate to have had three children born before the curse had been uttered. But now, of Kieran's children, only his son, Killian, remained alive.

Hugh often wished his father had related the exact wordage of the hex. Though a fearless warrior, Hugh had noticed the unmistakable consternation on his father's gaunt face when he had broached the subject. He had been completely unwilling to discuss it and had died only weeks after the encounter with the witch. Hugh only knew the O'Briens' line was to suffer the pain that had been forced upon her. He'd ordered her killed, hoping that would put an end to it, but she was elusive. Even the captain and his guard, the most bold and loyal of soldiers, feared the witch.

Once, he had attempted the deed himself and nearly been killed for his trouble.

Hugh headed his horse toward the fairy glade determined to find the witch, to put an end to this vexation that had been thrust upon his family. As he rounded the fairy glade he felt his usually calm steed lurch beneath him. He attempted to calm the horse, but he continued to dangerously rear and fiercely snort. Hugh lost all control of the beast and he felt himself being thrown viciously. The pain shot through his head as it struck a rock, leaving him unconscious. When he awoke, his leg lay twisted and bent, and the sorceress herself stood looking down upon him with a piercing stare.

Chapter Five

HER LONG, DARK hair billowed wildly in the wind. He had fought in many battles, faced many a formidable foe, but he had never before felt this kind of terror. He thought she would kill him, hoped she would only take his life, not his soul. But, she smiled wickedly.

He had known of her as a young woman. She had lived in the castle, been one of the servants. He'd thought her pleasant and quite beautiful. He wondered what event had changed her so markedly. Had she always had an evil within her?

"You wish to know why I have cursed you, O' Brien?" she hissed.

"Aye, I do, woman. What can be done to end this curse, to appease what wrong has been done to you?"

"When your line dies out entirely, or when my child is accepted as nobility by your line. When you see to it my child retains all that has been taken by your kin."

"But woman, your child is dim-witted!" he growled. He immediately regretted his impulsive words.

"Only then, O'Brien," she whispered over the heightening wind.

He heard a rustling in the bushes behind him and looked toward the fairy glade. He was not above believing the superstition, that if a human entered that glade he would be captured by the wickedest of fairies, but he thought at that moment it might be preferable. But, when the witch heard the stirring, he noticed fear in her eyes. She glanced over her shoulder at the chieftain one last time, her eyes blazing, and disappeared into the mist. His leg had healed well enough, though it ached fiercely on cold, damp days. He walked with a slight limp and found mounting his horse difficult.

But, it was not his body so greatly affected by the meeting with the witch, as his mind and his soul. He still awoke from his dreams in a cold sweat, filled with dread, knowing full well it had been the witch who plagued his dreams. He had never told a soul about his encounter with her. To this very day, it was thought he was simply thrown from his horse while out on a moonlit ride. Since then, he had learned to be content with his blessings and to pray no further misfortune would mar his family.

He could not for all his trying begin to understand why the witch thought her child with the disfigured body and ill-formed mind could be expected to live in the castle or be treated as nobility. Though he did not know the paternity of the child, and he had dwelled on that many a sleepless night, he could not make himself believe the father had been an O'Brien. Three of his brothers had been off in the neighboring province, fighting with O'Rorkes against the O'Byrnes, when the woman would have become with child. That only left Kieran, who lived far from here and was a contentedly married man, and Sean, his youngest brother who would have been scarcely more than a boy and already in love with the woman he later took as his wife.

Hugh himself might have looked at her appraisingly a time or two, for the witch had been a lovely maiden, at the time, but, in the early years of his marriage, he had remained faithful to his wife, Lady Siobhan. That left only his father and, though he might have been known to have a woman now and again, after Hugh's mother had died, he usually preferred frequenting the brothels in the neighboring harbor village. It was more discreet and made things less messy, he had explained to Hugh when questioned on it.

Hugh O'Brien gazed out from his position atop the north solar, at the picturesque hills in the distance and the mighty river that ran through his land. He enjoyed this time of the morning, before his duties took him to the great hall where he would sit for most of the day, dealing with manners brought to his attention by his captain, his steward, and his priest. There would be discussions, and he would declare his opinion or pass judgments. But, for now, he reveled in this time when he could be alone with his thoughts.

He was proud of this land, of this castle, and he prided himself in being fair and just. Leaning against the turret, he caught sight of the three lads out in the field beyond the moat. They practiced with the broadsword, this morning, and he watched with pride how capable they had become.

Riley knowledgably lifted his heavy sword above his head, spun about and crashed it down toward his brother, Rory. Rory, the swift-thinker dodged the blow, turned himself around and struck Riley's blade with an undercut that clashed distinctly and rang out loudly through the air. Both men laughed aloud at the swift exchange and continued on with their sparing.

Hugh chuckled to himself at the exchange. He would not care to challenge either of the young men for he doubted, in his increasing age, he could best them, any longer.

He looked closely at Riley, named for the O'Reillys, Hugh's mother's clan. He was the elder of his twin sons, though, in truth, only minutes older than his brother. His skin was dark like an O'Brien and his hair a mass of black curls often tied back from his face. He was tall, yet stocky of build. His features, more severe than those of his brother. He was a serious lad who relished the knowledge he would surely be chieftain one day. He pushed himself untiringly to become the best at everything he attempted, whether in sport, during a hunt, or in preparation for battle. Rory, named for his wife's clan, the O'Rorkes, was his brother's opposite in both appearance and disposition. His straight, honey-colored hair was inherited from his mother and her people. He was almost as tall as his brother, but of a slighter girth, and much more affable with a ready smile and gentle manner. His inclination was to be the carefree jester, quite pleased that it would most certainly be his brother who became chieftain. Although he possessed an apt intelligence of strategic matters, Rory disliked conflict of any kind and Hugh thought it fortunate they had not gone to battle for some time, for he feared it would cause Rory great displeasure. He preferred to keep the peace. He was skilled enough with the bow and the sword, and he had clearly surpassed Riley in scholarly studies. This was a great insult to the older twin, for his competitive nature impelled him to excel in whatever he attempted. Yet, despite their many differences, the twins remained close, even now, as adults.

And the third boy, Killian, his brother Kieran's only living descendant, was a pleasant mixture of his own two sons. He was taller than Riley, of a muscular build, but not so thick, and his hair was a dark, rich brown. He took his training seriously, but was perhaps more balanced than the twins. In truth, and he would only admit it to himself, Hugh believed Killian would make a more capable chieftain than either of his sons.

Though only a year older than the twins, Killian was a born leader. His strong political opinions could often sway many a man's way of thinking. He was well respected by the peasants, the nobles, and the guards. He had a natural eloquence in speaking that would surely rally many an allegiance and a level-headedness that would be a great quality in a chieftain. He was friendly and charming, but, when riled, he was a force to be reckoned with. His connection to the O'Donnel clan, his mother's people, would be most important in the years to come. They lived in the east-central area of Ireland, a strategic stronghold for battles against the English, so Killian was vital to keeping the O'Donnel allegiance.

He was very dear to Hugh on a personal level, as well. His father had been next to him in age and they had always been the closest of brothers and friends. Therefore, it was only natural that he adored this young man. He had survived a terrible ordeal when he was still a boy and seemed only stronger for it. He was a better swordsman than Riley, and, in truth, he doubted even the captain of the guard could oust him. He was more skilled at the bow than Rory and seldom came home empty-handed from a game hunt.

As Hugh stood looking at the lads, he noticed the girl, sitting in the herb garden. It didn't escape his notice how often the farrier's daughter could be found near the O'Brien lads. They were like bees to a flower. He remembered well what desires ruled young men, and she was a pretty sort. But, the girl was a mystery to him. Her beauty was rare, which in itself was odd. The old farrier was far from handsome, in truth, quite a homely man. He was large of build with facial features to match and his wife, who had died many years previous, had been plain at best. And, if his memory served him correctly, she had been obedient and meek. The farrier himself was also a quiet man. He was a loyal servant and a gifted horseman, remaining in charge of the clan's horses even at his advanced age.

The daughter, though, was talkative and spoke her mind more than a woman should, especially one of lowly birth. She had been allowed privileges most of common blood would never know. Ever since she had aided in the healing of his nephew, he noticed how often she was allowed in the castle whether with old Morag or his own sons and nephew. Hugh's own wife, Lady Siobhan, had a giant soft spot for the girl. She said it was because she reminded her of her younger sister who had died when she was just a girl. He believed it may be her great want of a daughter and that the girl had no mother. They had formed a bond the chieftain was not entirely pleased about.

His wife had insisted, against his better judgment, that the girl be allowed time with the scholar, since she was such a bright child. He recalled how displeased Riley had been. He was insulted that the girl, a commoner no less, could take learning with the chieftain's kin. It was true the captain's son had taken lessons with them, for it had been proven that advanced learning often led to better strategies when planning battles and instructing soldiering. And, the cook's son needed schooling in order to put the many directions and ingredients to ink.

His wife had pointed out how beneficial it would be to have the girl learn to write so she might catalogue Morag's potions and remedies. The woman was very old and it was unlikely she would live long. He clearly recalled the conversation.

"Hugh O'Brien, Morag is nearly ancient, sure she cannot be expected to live so very much longer. And when she passes is she to take all knowledge of her potions and cures along with her? Allow the girl to learn the way of putting the remedies to ink!"

"A girl child? A commoner? The farrier's daughter taking schooling with the O'Brien lads?" he scoffed.

"And the cook's son and the captain of the guard's son, as well," she reminded him.

"But all males nonetheless?"

The woman determinedly searched for a way to change her husband's mind.

"Then allow her lessons alone with the scholar."

"Surely you jest! Private lessons? On whose coin, woman? 'Tis unheard of!"

"So be it then, Hugh, allow old Morag to pass on, and with her take all the knowledge of her healing. And when your kin or your sons or your wife go to the beyond for lack of a proper remedy, sure you must take comfort in knowing the farrier's daughter was not allowed schooling with our sons by your word!"

He had cussed under his breath knowing there was clearly no way to win this argument with his clever wife. And so the girl had been schooled. It was thought the girl might only take lessons for a short term, but, when it was discovered how much more diligent Riley, who struggled with his lessons, and all the lads had become in trying to ensure the girl did not exceed their scores, the chieftain relented and allowed her to continue with the studying. The scholar, who initially had been opposed to teaching a female, was both shocked and amazed at what a quick study she had been. He'd told the earl he believed her thirst for knowledge was greater than any other student he had schooled.

But, Hugh drew the line when his sons and nephew wanted her to attend the royal celebrations. He'd encountered many an argument from his wife in this regard, but he had not relented, having no desire to set precedent with commoners attending his feasts when lords and ladies were present. He had told his kin it would be cruel to have the girl subjected to judgment from those of a higher class and, though she may have had some learning, she was clearly not of their breeding or social standing. She was, after all, a servant, no matter how beautiful and seemingly intelligent she might be.

The loud clang of a sword hitting the ground and laughter of his sons interrupted his thoughts momentarily, but he was drawn once more to the girl and his eyes lingered upon her appraisingly.

If he was the sort of man to keep a mistress, she would be a tempting sort. Her hair always shimmered most lustrously. Even in her dull, loose frock, she was the most sensuous young woman he had looked upon in an age. He doubted there was a man in the county who hadn't envisioned bedding her. He flushed as he imagined her sitting astride him in his bed. The thought had no sooner crossed his mind, when she looked up, from her place in the garden, her eyes meeting his. He was certain they held an accusing stare, unsettling him more than he would have imagined. He stepped back from the window, angered at the shame she'd caused him to feel. He thought it best she be married off soon. It would surely not be difficult to find a man who would agree to it. Aye, when his sons' coming of age celebrations were completed, he would see to it that the distraction of the farrier's daughter was rectified. He would have her wed as soon as it could be arranged.

⌘

WITH SOME DIFFICULTY, Alainn disconnected her mind from the chieftain's thoughts. The dizziness took over, again, and she felt as though she were falling. When the world finally stilled, she opened her eyes and was relieved to be looking upon the garden, once more.

She heard the sound of the chieftain's sons sparring, the swords clashing, their laughter as the sword clanged and fell to the ground. She heard the distinctive call of the dove, the cawing of the crow. Again!

Instinctively, she once more glanced up at the north solar and looked at the chieftain. She dropped her head in fear and despair, not at the chieftain's thoughts, but the look they had shared. Again! Had she somehow altered time? It was as though she were reliving all that had happened just moments earlier. She had experienced this before. The chieftain's sons were now speaking the exact same words, but all sounds seemed far away, echoing unnaturally.

She should have listened to Morag more intently, obeyed her more diligently. The old woman had told her she may have magical abilities she was not aware of and that she may very well become incapable of controlling her powers if she insisted on developing them further. Alainn shook her head and felt as though she might lose consciousness. She could remember scattered bits and pieces of the chieftain's thoughts, but they were muddled and confusing. Her head pounded, her stomach lurched, and she thought she would spew. In the din, she heard the chieftain's nephew calling her name.

Chapter Six

"ALAINN!" SHE GLANCED up to see the chieftain's nephew a few feet away, leaning against the dry-stone wall that enclosed the herb garden, staring at her with concern.

Accustomed to keeping her abilities secretive, she knew she could not tell Killian she had used her powers or any of what she had learned. He was fiercely protective of her, as he would have been to his own sister had she lived. He did not know how often Alainn called upon her powers and he most certainly had no inkling of how many men she had fought off to keep her virtue intact. She would not want him to feel he had to battle every man who looked at her.

Though she appreciated his concern, he often treated her like a child. Killian O'Brien seemed to have missed the fact that she had become a woman, and Alainn found herself growing angry, even knowing how unreasonable it was. She distracted herself of all that had just transpired by returning to the old sore subject they had been discussing before she and the chieftain had locked minds.

"I see no reason why you refuse to teach me the way of

wielding a sword, Killian O'Brien."

He appeared momentarily perplexed by her slow response and pallid complexion, but hearing her comment he
grinned at her and continued their usual banter.

"Well, Alainn McCreary," he taunted, " 'tis a dangerous
task and not one to be attempted by a woman. And, I would
think after the last incident, when a lesson involved a blade,
you wouldn't even consider asking me this."

"That was nearly four years ago and barely more than a
scratch."

"I had to pull the anelace from your chest, Alainn! You
lost a good deal of blood and scared me fiercely. And, had it
been a finger's width lower, you'd be missin' a vital area
you'll need for nourishing the babes you'll have one day.
Pierce had no business trying to show you how to manage
such maneuvers!" Killian shook his head, vividly recalling
that day.

He'd been out in the adjacent field practicing soldiering
with his cousins. They were in mock battle with a sparth axe
when he'd heard the scream. He'd known immediately it was
Alainn, injured, and, though he'd never moved so fast, it
seemed an eternity to get to her. She had crumpled to her
knees, the dagger protruding from her chest. Pierce, the
captain of the guards' son, a boy no older than she, stood by
her, wearing an expression of horror and shame. The blood
had seeped through her frock and she was shivering. Her face
had grown deathly pale.

Riley was directly behind him, cussing by his ear. Rory, farther off, yelled for Pierce to mount his horse and go fetch Morag. Killian dropped to his knees beside her and tore open her dress and undergarment to assess the damage. The knife had lodged in her right breast, just above the nipple. Even in her obvious pain and despair, she tried to cover herself, displeased that he had seen her recently blossomed breasts, and he could think of nothing to do, bar removing the weapon.

It was a thin dagger, of which he was pleased, but an anelace. Though a most effective weapon, it had a double-edged blade ensuring a most painful removal. He placed his body between her and the young men, further pulled back the garments, and, looking into her eyes with empathy, yanked it from her flesh. She screamed, again, but did not lose consciousness, as he had when he had once suffered the blade of such a weapon.

He quickly ripped a strip off his own tunic and, holding it tight to her wound, picked her up in his arms. Though still winded from his previous sprint, he ran with her to Morag. He had refused to leave her side the entire time the healer attended Alainn's wound. Even though the aged woman had ordered him to go, he stood his ground and made certain she would live.

"You hang on to grudges for too long, Killian O'Brien." Her words pulled him from thoughts of that day. " 'Twas not the captain's son to blame. Sure, he was not agreeable to it, but I convinced him to do so, as I called in a favor."

"Aye, I know well enough you are most persuasive, and Pierce has always been smitten with you. So, I doubt it took much convincin'."

"He has been known to hang about me a time or two."

"He fawns over ye like flies to a dung pile."

"Such a lovely comparison, Killian O'Brien. Now, I'm liken to a dung pile, am I?"

" 'Twas not my meaning. I was only pointing out the fact that he's his eye on you."

"Aye, he has written me lovely poems telling me such."

"He writes you poems? Christ! He must be worse off than I thought."

"Now, you are indicating having feelings for me is foolish?"

"That's not what I'm implyin', either! You should not encourage the lad, though, Alainn. He may be prone to make improper advances toward you."

"And, maybe I would not consider them so improper. Pierce has grown into a most handsome young man. He's tall and strong and surely brave, being the captain's son. Perhaps, I might choose to make advances toward him should I take a notion." She smiled prettily at Killian and batted her eyelashes in an inviting manner, pushing her chest forward.

Killian was clearly not amused. "You can stop that, here and now. You'll not encourage him in any manner, for I think it would not take much on your part to have him thinkin' he could have his way with you, and, aye, he's plenty strong enough to manage it, I'd wager."

"Pierce would never hurt me," she insisted.

"You don't know the ways of men, Alainn."

"How can you be so certain of that?"

His jaw tightened and his eyes narrowed as he closed the distance, crouching beside her as he spoke. "Do not make light of such things, Alainn. Virtue is most important in women and an important feature to a man when choosin' a wife. And, you cannot toy with men in that regard. They don't take kindly to being taunted and often take what they believe is being offered, even if the woman isn't truly in favor of it. You're a rare beauty, and you have a way of charmin' a man into doing things he would not normally do. So, I'll instruct you to not mislead men, and that is the last I would like heard of such matters. As to the matter of you handlin' a sword, I forbid it!"

Her azure eyes flashed in rebellious fury at his words and his tone. "You cannot order me about, Killian O'Brien! By what right do you feel you can tell me what I may or may not do? If I want to learn the use of the sword, I will find someone who will show me. Mark my words. I will!"

"You possess a stubborn streak that exceeds even your beauty! I know you are an intelligent girl. Think of the workings of the sword. It is a powerfully heavy weapon. You are a girl of fine build. You don't possess the physical strength necessary to wield the weapon. The saber, perhaps, but not the broadsword."

"You underestimate my strength, but, teach me the ways of the saber, then, if you think that would suit me better," she demanded. "You still owe me a favor, Killian O'Brien."

"If you're speaking of your healin' me all those years ago, I think that debt has been paid, in truth, several times. I managed to get you to Morag in time to save you, though I might have allowed you to bleed to death if I'd known how difficult you'd become as you grew older! And, there are a dozen other favors I've done for you. Didn't I convince my aunt to allow you to be schooled by the same scholar the O'Briens employ? You know how rare it is to have a female taught to read and write and do figures, even a female of noble blood."

"Which, I am not!" Her teeth clenched. "You needn't remind me of that. Morag tells me so nearly every day."

"You may be born of commoners, but you're certainly not common," he growled. "Even without the magic, and, besides, I did teach you to use the longbow and helped you learn how to handle a horse."

"Aye, and I have become most astute at both."

"As with everything," he bantered.

"Don't mock me, Killian O'Brien!" She glared defiantly, arms crossing.

"It has been years since you healed me, Alainn," he said impatiently. "I've given in to your whims more times than I could count and been chastised by many in the doing. My uncle has not yet forgiven me for the time I hid you behind the curtain in the great hall. He was enraged to learn a woman had been present during the proceedings of his court. Rules are to be strictly adhered to and I knew full well females are only allowed presence in that room during feasts and celebrations."

"Aye, but we can look down upon the judgments through the peephole in the room above, and he knows of this. He must presume females are so dense we are unable to understand the happenings or so distrustful we might spread rumors. I don't take kindly to being suspected of either."

"He hopes to shelter women from some of the unpleasant happenings that take place within. The lashings are not a sight for a lady to behold and I swear the sound of it is even more disturbing. 'Tis perhaps a kindness to womenfolk that they are spared the sound of a subject begging for mercy or screaming while being hauled off to a stay in the dungeon. In truth, you should be thankful to him, Alainn, for it is not always so desirous to be a part of that."

"Aye, well there were no lashings the day I was there."

"Blessed be that you were found out after only an hour or so."

"Aye, well it was a dreadful dusty curtain I hid behind, and I had to force myself not to sneeze more than once. I even stifled a scream when the rat ran over my foot, but when it became entangled in my skirts I could not for the life of me stop myself. And, you would defend your uncle in any decision he might make, Killian O'Brien."

"You make it sound like an accusation, Alainn. I am loyal to the O'Brien. He is a wise man and a good chieftain."

Though she thought she agreed, for the most part, Hugh O'Brien's unsavory thoughts still filled her ears. And now, she would have to contend with the chieftain's plans to have her wed.

"Alainn, we have been friends throughout all these years and, still, you will not simply call me by my given name."

"It is not proper for commoners to refer to your noble family with such familiarity, and you treat me not as a friend but a lecturer. You used to be much more pleasant to be with!"

"Don't be cross with me for being an O'Brien or not allowing you to learn the way of the sword, Alainn. It is for your own good. You would only injure yourself, and you've far too pretty a face to chance marring it."

Alainn snorted in response. "If it had been a sword you'd been toying with that day, you may well have had that lovely wee breast lopped off."

Her cheeks turned pinker still. "Save that talk for the miller's daughter, Killian O'Brien," she exploded, "for 'tis her breasts you seem to have such an affinity for!"

"Christ, Alainn, it was nearly two years ago you happened upon us behind the stables, and still you flay me for it!" He edged closer to her and gently pinched her cheek as he'd done since she was a child. Her blue eyes fumed at the gesture.

It made it more difficult now that he had grown so handsome in these ten years. His shoulders and chest were broad and muscular. His waist, tapered and narrow. Extremely tall, he towered over her when they stood together. She looked up. Rich chestnut hair fell to his shoulders in a most appealing manner, framing his rugged face, with its high cheekbones and strong nose and chin. His lips were full, and his teeth, straight and white. But it was Killian O'Brien's eyes that captured her heart most. They had not faded in his adulthood. They were as brilliant and captivating as ever and, though his face could often conceal his mood or thoughts, his eyes could not. His mirth was always present in his deep green eyes but so, too, was his ire.

Alainn knew him well. They'd been friends since the day she'd come to him, so many years before, and they'd spent countless hours together, speaking of things kept only between them. Even though Killian and his cousins were older than Alainn, they had allowed her to tag along more times than not, and it was true she had been allowed to be taught lessons with them. She had delighted in that and would be ever grateful to Killian for insisting upon it, and to Lady Siobhan O'Brien for agreeing, despite the chieftain's hesitations.

She had been allowed many opportunities through the years that other girls, especially girls of her station, had not. And, it was not only schooling she had enjoyed and excelled at. She had become as proficient as the lads at riding a horse, the only characteristic she might have adopted from her father. And, she could climb a tree as nimbly, even with long skirts to hamper her.

Alainn had fond memories of playing in the castle, in the many immense rooms, alcoves, and stairways, which proved to be wonderful areas for games and challenges. She'd skinned her knees and elbows as often as the lads and had adored the freedom to frolic in the meadows and the stone close beyond the castle.

She considered Rory, the good-natured O'Brien twin, her friend as well. They shared a common sense of humor and were often chastised by Riley, the far more serious boy, for their foolishness. Riley had never been in favor of including her, because of her gender and breeding, but he had given up protesting, knowing he was outnumbered. She recalled how angry Riley had become when she continually won the races up the steps of the narrow, winding tower. He suggested she might wear heavy boots, as the boys did, objecting that her tiny slippers allowed her to make it to the top so swiftly. She had told him she would be pleased to wear the heavy boots if he would agree to don her many layers of skirts. The other boys hooted at her saucy retort, and Riley's face had turned bright red.

"You are deep in thought, Lainna," Killian said, calling her by his pet name, given her so many years before.

"Nothing of consequence," she answered, picking up her

basket of greens, "but I am due back at the kitchen with the herbs for Cook's soup and Morag's remedies." He offered his hand but she would not meet his eyes. It was much easier to be angry with him, to be bickering. For, when she looked into his eyes, she felt weak at the knees. When she was near him, her body ached with a longing to be held, and she was certain he did not share those thoughts. Though she could hear the thoughts of many, Killian's seldom came to her. It infuriated her more than she cared to admit that he still saw her as a child, and she felt undeniably hurt when he spent time with other women. She'd been mortified the day she'd caught him with the miller's daughter, embarrassed, humiliated, and more jealous than she'd known she could ever be.

"Why are you always at odds with me, Alainn?" Killian murmured. "We once had such lengthy conversations, such happy times. You used to tell me your thoughts. As of late, you always seem to be in a temper."

" 'Tis because of the way you treat me, Killian O'Brien," she complained. "My father may not act the part, but I don't require you to father me. I am no longer a child!"

Chapter Seven

"I KNOW IT well enough, Alainn," he sighed. He was most definitely aware she had reached maturity. He was a man, after all, and she was an indescribably beautiful woman. He could scarcely keep his eyes off her, though he tried to keep his mind from dishonorable thoughts. Even now, as she'd bent to pick up her supplies, he had to fight his desire to imagine her well-formed backside without skirts to hide it. And, he hadn't missed how the apron of her frock could not conceal her high, firm breasts. He'd seen them that once but was too fearful to take much notice, and she'd matured since that day.

For years, he would wake from his sleep and know he had dreamed an erotic dream involving Alainn. He'd feel deeply ashamed, for she was younger at that time. He no longer felt shame for dreaming of her, but it did unsettle him in a way he did not care for and he was fiercely displeased if anyone else admitted thinking of her in this way. He knew well enough how possessive he had become. But, there was little use in having any expectations beyond friendship, for they were of very different worlds. Try as he might, he couldn't keep away from her, though, at times, he truly had attempted it. When he pulled himself from his thoughts, he noticed she was halfway to the courtyard. He lengthened his stride to catch up with her.

"I recognize the fact you are a woman, Alainn. I am neither blind nor unintelligent."

She huffed and tossed her head haughtily. They had no time to conclude their personal conversation, as they were joined by the O'Brien lads and the captain of the guard's son, Pierce. They walked toward the castle with Riley and Pierce leading the way and Killian and Rory flanking her. Alainn frowned in displeasure when the steward's sons joined the group.

Henry, the older, was an abrasive sort and Alainn did not care for him in the least. She had threatened him with her dagger on more than one occasion when he attempted to familiarize himself with what lay beneath her frock. His brother, Richard, though the younger of the two and barely older than herself, was even more unlikable. He had a mean streak within him, taking unnatural pleasure in being cruel to younger children and animals. Alainn had made a bad enemy of him when she was ten and two. One day, when she was walking to the dog pens where the chieftain kept his prized Irish wolfhounds, she noticed an empty pen. On hearing painful yelps in a nearby thicket, she had run to investigate and, upon entering the brush, saw a sight so disturbing, she still thought of it. The horrid boy had tied the dog to a tree and was burning him with a flaming branch. The dog's hair had been burned off and its flesh was smoldering. It looked near death and Alainn had screamed at the sight.

The loathsome boy seemed to delight in her fear and disgust. She had run toward him and he'd threatened her with the blazing wood. So compelled was she by her rage and revulsion, her witchcraft had taken over. The stick was sent flying from his hands and into the nearby stream. He had gaped in disbelief but charged toward the dog to kick it. Alainn held out her hand and the boy froze, unable to move. Rage shone in his eyes, spurring him to fight the unseen force holding him back.

Alainn withdrew her power, purposely flinging him toward a boulder. His head hit the rock with a sickening thud, and she had to fight the desire to have the boulder roll on top of him. He lay unconscious as Alainn felt the power humming in her veins and battled the will to take his life. She was repulsed to find herself reveling in the power.

Pulling her thoughts from the boy, she looked to the animal whimpering on the ground beside her. She bent and laid her hands to its wounds, tears pouring down her cheeks the whole while. Though she could not repair the damaged fur, she watched the wounds heal within moments. The dog looked up with grateful brown eyes and soon appeared to regain its strength. When she released it from its tether, the dog ran at the boy, baring its teeth. The animal turned back as if to get her permission to tear his assailant to shreds. Alainn wanted to give it, and what frightened her more than the wanting was the knowledge that she hungered to watch it. Could it be so different than watching a criminal hanged for his wrongdoings?

Alainn fought the battle and would never know what path she might have chosen, for the boy came to and the dog grabbed hold of his arm, ripping at it. One of the chieftain's guards came upon them and was horrified at the scene. He was about to kill the animal when Alain intervened, telling the man that the boy had been torturing it and the dog had only retaliated.

She never disclosed the degree of the crime, for she would have been forced to tell her part in it, and the wounds were nearly healed. The guard, clearly unsure what to believe, decided on clemency for the dog and the healer's attention for the boy. To this day, Alainn avoided the boy, now a man, though she thought he feared her. She couldn't deny that she feared him, as well.

The black cloud that enshrouded him was as dark as Alainn had ever seen. It could only be an ominous sign that Richard McGilvary grew more evil each day. He also made no attempt to hide his contempt for her. She knew, though it was the dog that mauled him, he attributed his misfortune to her. Even now, he did not have total function of his once mangled arm. Alainn could not make herself feel remorseful about that.

She'd told Killian part of what had happened, and the chieftain soon after had padlocks put on the dogs' cages. She shivered, remembering the horrible day. It was the closest she had ever felt to being evil, herself. Killian touched her arm and she looked into his concerned eyes. She could only shake her head at his unspoken questions.

When they reached the courtyard, they met up with Cook's son and Alainn welcomed the sight of the cheerful young man.

"Good Morning, Alainn, Killian! Glorious day, is it not?"

Cook's son, whose name was usually condensed to Cookson, had pale grey eyes that were always filled with merriment. His temperament was even. His manner, jesting. Both traits were much appreciated in the busy hustle and bustle of the hot and, humid kitchen.

Although both the cook and his son had given names, they were always fondly referred to as Cook and Cookson. Both large men, with more than ample meat on their bones, their happy natures and hearty, contagious laughs made the kitchen a wonderful place to spend a day.

Not only was the cook wonderful at his trade, producing dozens of delicious meals for the entire castle with the assistance of his large staff, he was also the closest thing to a real father Alainn had ever known. He had a large family, thirteen children in all, his baker's dozen, as everyone called them, to which he would proudly retort that he was not simply a baker but the head-cook of the entire O'Brien castle. Alainn had shared many a meal at their home, seated at their enormous table, surrounded by their genuine affection.

She adored Cook's wife, Margaret. As plump as her husband, when she grabbed you to her ample bosom for a motherly embrace, there was no doubt you were loved. Alainn had often thought, if she could have been born unto another family, she would gladly be one of Cook's children.

There were only three daughters in Cook's brood. One of them, Molly, was Alainn's only true female friend. She was younger than Alainn and timid, with shiny red hair that hung about her face in lovely ringlets that Alainn had always envied. Molly did not spend time with her when she was with the O'Brien lads. Morag said it was because that girl knew her place, but Alainn thought it was just her nature to prefer to do more ladylike activities.

She adored sitting at home and doing fine needlework with her mother. Alainn found sewing completely mundane but admired the beautiful pieces both women were capable of creating. Though Molly was a quiet girl, when they were together, she often confided her female desires. Even if Alainn had a fancy toward Pierce, she would never have followed through with it, as Molly was clearly infatuated with the captain's son. Cookson often jested with his sister regarding her affection toward Pierce. Her cheeks would turn a fiery red and she would smile shyly.

It puzzled many as to why Morag's young assistant spent a good portion of her time in the kitchen, but Cook had noted the girl's talent for growing herbs for remedies and had enlisted her in growing and sorting herbs for cooking. He had little time to tend to the size of the herb garden needed to make the assortment of dishes required for the chieftain and his family. When Alainn wasn't with Morag, administering herbal potions to the sick or injured, she was helping out in the kitchen or tending to the herbs. Morag's stooped, aching back would no longer allow her to work in the garden. Alainn had gladly taken over that part of Morag's chores.

Deep in thought, Alainn scarcely noticed that the two groups of young men had divided. Killian, Rory, and Cookson were discussing the repair of a wobbly wheel on Cookson's cart. They had tipped over the cart and were presently deciding whether they could tend to the wheel themselves or if they must take it to the cart-maker.

The conversation between the other young men assailed her ears and infuriated her. She bit her tongue to keep from adding her opinion. She had dropped her head and started toward the kitchen, an angry look upon her face, when the eldest McGilvary boy directed a colorful comment toward her. She turned and glared, trying desperately not to speak her mind. Killian and Cookson had their backs turned, completely engrossed in the task of removing the wheel.

"You're looking a bit flushed this morning, Alainn

McCreary," Riley taunted. "Do you object to our discussion? Or has the topic warmed your usual frigidity?"

"Aye, I object to it. You might keep such matters limited to a private place. I've no desire to hear details of your latest debauchery."

"Then, you needn't eavesdrop," Riley countered.

"But, I am standing not two feet from you. If you must regale the men folk with your most recent conquest, you might at least be decent enough to make sure there is no female in your company."

"You can leave if you don't take kindly to it, for this does not involve you," said Henry, the steward's eldest son.

"Aye, 'tis not really your concern, Alainn McCreary," Riley continued, " 'tis not as if we're boasting to having bedded you, though I'm sure it has crossed all of our minds on more than a few occasions." The three young men snickered.

"You are truly an incorrigible man, Riley O'Brien, and it is my concern when you speak so disrespectfully of females. It is most definitely disconcerting to me! You might at least attempt anonymity when boasting about a woman. Must you sully her name, too? You think, because you are men, you can belittle and degrade women to your liking. It appalls me!"

"I'll not apologize to you for being a man and rejoicing in that fact, Alainn McCreary. I assure you, her name was sullied even before I had a go with her, and you would do best to remember you are simply a farrier's daughter, a servant to my kin. You have no right to pass judgment on me. If I want to shag every woman in the entire countryside, it is my right."

"Because you are a man you feel you can use them and discard them at your choosing!" Alainn spit out.

"Aye, well I may have used them, but I've not had any complaints. They've seemed quite willing by the time we have completed the joining and many have come back for more."

"And, what choice do they have, you sot? They are your subjects, and you, the man one day to be chieftain. You're a large, strong man of noble birth, you can take what you will. And, I seriously doubt they all enjoyed the deed, though they would surely not relate to you the humiliation and terror they feel at having a man force themselves on them!"

"You're insinuating I rape them, are you?"

"Aye, 'tis rape when you know they only agree to it because of your position."

"And, there are many a position they seem to agree to," he boasted arrogantly.

Killian moved toward his cousin. "Sure, 'tis enough, Riley. You'd be wise to close your mouth."

"Aye, 'tis not the place," Rory agreed.

"Why? Because, the wee farrier's daughter might be insulted by our topic? The two of you have boasted about women in just such a fashion. You're only more secretive about it since you seem to value her opinion. I do not give a tinker's damn what she thinks of me, and if I want to speak about this I will do so. She'll not dictate any part of my life. And, if I should desire to take her out behind the pig shed and do what I will with her, there is little she could do about it!"

"Then, you would be fornicating with a corpse, you vile ingrate! For, only if I were dead, would you be capable of accomplishing that. Or, perhaps that is something you take pleasure in as well!" She flew at him in a rage, her nails raking his cheek, her fists pounding his chest.

Rory grabbed hold of her and pulled her off. Killian gripped the scruff of Riley's tunic and snarled, "And, it would be over my dead body, as well, for I am not intimidated by the fact you are to be chieftain one day."

Alainn shook herself out of Rory's grasp, hot angry tears brimming in her eyes. She clenched her hands as the steward's sons ogled her. Of all the men in the chieftain's service, she despised those two most for her powers of perception had shown what indecencies they had committed toward women. Her anger reached an unusual level and she fought to control her powers. Killian tried to take her arm but she pulled away from him. "You're all guilty of degrading women, the lot of you!"

"Not me, Alainn," Cookson teased, trying to disperse the tension. "My father says being with one woman was good enough for him and it will be for me, as well, so I am to keep any thought of women in that regard far back in me mind."

Riley laughed heartily. Richard, the youngest of the steward's sons, sneered, "You're so bloody heavy you'd be likely to crush any woman you attempted to bed."

Alainn shook with rage. "You are the vilest of men, Richard McGilvary! You are not only insensitive to women, you are cruel and abusive, and I think the chieftain would be wise to toss you in the dungeon and throw away the key before you add murder to your list of indecencies!"

"Aye, well, if I was to murder a woman it would be you at the top of the list! You, who thinks yourself above the rest of us common folk because you can read and write. Reading and writing will be of little good when you are wed to one of us lowly peasants and expected to submit to a man's needs every time he desires it. Sure, it would be fitting if it is me you find atop you in a marriage bed."

"I'd as soon throw myself in a vat of pure lye, you filthy, loathsome creature!"

"Alainn, just stop this!" Killian ordered. "Be quiet now and let me handle this."

"I will not stop, Killian O'Brien! I intend to be heard, for I will speak for all women who are so oppressed they cannot. Men expect their intended to be virginal, yet they go about deflowering every woman they desire!"

Rory O'Brien defended himself. "I have never deflowered a maiden, Alainn. 'Tis only harlots I've been intimate with and they were well compensated for their efforts."

"But 'tis still a dishonor to women, Rory!" Alainn cried, throwing up her hands in exasperation. "Would it be so unimaginable for both the husband and wife to be virginal on the wedding night, as Cookson suggested?"

"It might be beneficial for one of them to know what's to be done," Killian growled, looking to be at the edge of his patience.

"I expect they would figure it out eventually," she retorted. "Cook and his wife seem to have gotten along well enough, being as they have thirteen children."

"Jesus, Mary, and Joseph!" stormed Riley. "She's not our mother or our priest, and we're nobility! She's scarcely of higher breeding than the horses her father tends. You needn't explain or defend our rights as men. If you can't keep your wee charge quiet, Killian, she might find a fist in her wee mouth!"

Killian grabbed Alainn by the upper arm and began ushering her toward the castle, when Henry McGilvary crudely added, "If you want to prevent a woman from speaking, I know of something else other than a fist in the mouth that accomplishes it extremely well."

Killian released Alainn and withdrew his sword from its scabbard. The McGilvary lad lowered his eyes and stepped back. Killian held the weapon out toward his cousin clearly inviting him to duel.

Chapter Eight

"YOU WOULD FIGHT me, over the likes of her?" Riley queried.

"Aye, I would."

Riley's expression showed rage and disbelief as he glared at his cousin. "Now, there would only be a handful of reasons why you might do that. Either, you're planning to bed her yourself, or you mean to wed her. If you plan to bed her, you'd best take care, for she's obviously a wild cat." He touched his cheek where she'd torn it open in her rage. "And, if you plan to wed her, you can forget any chance of ever becoming a chieftain, for she'll not be accepted as a chieftain's wife when she has no title. You'll gain no allegiances with the clans, and she would surely produce inferior children." Alainn's blue eyes blazed with fury.

"Why should children be of consequence to an O'Brien. Until the curse is lifted, what difference could that possibly make?" she hissed. The noise and commotion turned to absolute silence, for, never, was anyone to speak aloud of the curse. "And, none of you need worry about whom I marry," she added in a softer tone, "for I intend to join a nunnery as soon as it can be arranged."

Cookson and Rory smiled at her words, but no one else moved a muscle. Killian's eyes grew dark, and his jaw, rigid. When Alainn thought the day could scarcely become worse, the castle's priest charged as fast as his cane would allow him, toward their gathering. She thought her rash declaration of becoming a nun was not a possibility if she would be made to associate with the likes of him.

"What is the meaning of this disturbance?" he wheezed, the vein in his bald head bulging. No one answered the man, and he grew impatient. "Who has caused this tumultuousness?"

"It was nothing, Father," Rory answered, "just a misunderstanding. It has been rectified."

The stern-faced man glanced at Killian.

"Aye, Father," he said, sheathing his sword. "It was only a disagreement between young people. We have worked it out."

"A dangerous one, I must conclude, if it resulted in near sword play." He looked pointedly at Riley's hand, which rested still on the hilt of his sword. "Perhaps, it would be best if I call the captain or his guardsmen?"

Pierce, the captain's son was quick to discourage that consideration. "No, 'tis smoothed over, Father," Pierce said quickly. "Most assuredly."

Still, the clergyman looked at Riley, as he had yet to speak his part. Rory and Killian both threw him furious glances for stalling in answering the man. Riley touched his raw cheek once more and frowned at Alainn but finally relented. "Aye, we'll not be needin' to call the guards."

Just then, the voice of Richard McGilvary called out, "It was the farrier's daughter, Father! She viciously attacked the chieftain's son. Take a look at his face." The priest whirled around and sneered at the girl before examining the lad's wounds. He started when he saw the torn, bloody skin. When McGilvary saw the priest's reaction, he continued, "She caused the rift between the chieftain's kin and has spoken aloud of the curse."

The priest stared with disdain at the farrier's daughter, taking his time before saying in a low and, menacing voice, "What do you have to say for yourself, girl?"

Alainn's mouth was dry with fear, for she knew the punishment for harming one of noble blood or speaking of the curse was at least a week's stay in the dungeon. Before she could find her tongue, Riley spoke again. "She was justified in lashing out at me. I was discourteous and spoke improperly toward her. My cousin only defended her good name." Her jaw dropped in surprise.

The priest looked doubtful but could hardly question the word of the chieftain's oldest son. He eyed the girl suspiciously. "And, what of the mention of the curse?"

This time Riley lied completely and Alainn knew not what to make of it. "I brought it up. She was only responding to my question."

"And, what was the question you directed to her?"

"I asked her if she would like me to curse her as our family has been cursed."

The old man drew back in shock. "You threatened to curse her?"

"Aye, well, I was sorely tempered at the time for my face was stinging so feckin' badly!"

"To be sure," the priest said, turning red at the colorful language. "And what was your response to his question, girl?" He looked annoyed at having to speak to her.

Alainn prided herself in never speaking untruths, but she strained her mind to come up with a response that would not cause the man to further scrutinize her.

"She really hadn't time to reply," Riley intervened.

The priest stared hard at her as if still expecting a response from her.

She hesitantly nodded.

"In future you would do best to mind your tongue and your temper, and don't tempt or provoke the chieftain's kin. Next time, a stay in the dungeon might be necessary."

"Aye, I'll see to it, Father," she agreed.

"Your fathers shall all be alerted to this incident," he sputtered. Glancing once more at the girl, he added, "And, the healer as well." With that, he set his crooked walking stick in position and hobbled away.

The crowd relaxed with relief to see the old man leave, except the steward's son, who wore a look of disappointment. Alainn threw him a nasty glare. Killian looked at him with equal disdain, then roughly grabbed Alainn's elbow and steered her away from the rest of the group. "You will meet me this evening at the usual place," he ordered.

She knew he meant the enormous dolmen where they had once spent many an hour alone together. She could not remember the last time they had been there. It had been at least two years, perhaps longer. Noticing the angry look within his emerald eyes, she began to protest. "I am not certain I will be able to slip out. Morag keeps close watch of me."

"Aye, well, the old crone is nearly blind and deaf, and you managed it well enough all those years when you were a child," he snarled. "You will find a way."

She opened her mouth to argue further, but thought better of it. Killian promptly escorted her to the kitchen gate and left without another word.

⌘

COOKSON FOLLOWED ALAINN into the kitchen. His cheeks were bright red. "Jesus, Mary, and Joseph, Alainn, I thought I might shite meself when the priest came upon that unpleasant scene. You've made a rather bad enemy of the man, I'd wager."

"I know it well enough, Cookson."

"And why does Richard McGilvary have it out for you? Though he's always been a nasty sort, he was clearly hopin' to get you punished."

She nodded her agreement, then, glanced over to the adjoining room where Morag sat on her wooden stool. It had only been recently that the old woman sat to do her duties. At one time, she refused to take the comfort of a chair. Now, she had little choice, for her frail body would not permit her to stand for any length of time. Alainn decided it was best she speak to the woman before the priest got to her first. There was a time, not so long ago, when she would have feared the lengthy lecture she would get from the old woman, but age and failing health had mellowed her, and, now, Alainn only regretted having to cause her concern.

"You must learn to control your tongue, caileag leanabh!" was the elderly woman's response when Alainn had related the day's happenings. Since the day she had come to live with the woman, who'd been old, even then, she had never called her Alainn. She always called her caileag leanabh, which was Gaelic for girl-child.

"You'll not change what has always been, just by not fancyin' it."

"But, women are treated so unfairly, Morag!"

"I know it well enough, but 'tis the way of it, and there's naught to be done about it." Alainn knew Morag spoke the truth, but the unfairness of the situation made her seethe inside. "And nearly scratchin' the chieftain's son's eyes out will accomplish nothin' but gettin' you in dire trouble. Though there's not been a woman hanged here in this castle, there have been women lashed and thrown in the dungeon. And, they are oft ostracized, ever after. You're mostly a good girl, and I'd not care to see you hurt in such a way. The priest may not be as righteous as he claims to be, but he has the chieftain's ear, and it would be foolish to draw any further attention to yerself. Just mind your ways for a time! I'm certain you're soon to be wed, if you haven't frightened off any suitors you might have by your unladylike behavior, today. And when you have a man to rule over you, it will be for the best."

"But, I don't want to be wed, and I most certainly do not want a man to rule over me!"

"In truth, ye've no choice in the matter, caileag. It is the way of it. In the end, nothin' you or I might want is of consequence."

"Oh, Morag, it angers me so. And, when I become that angry, I must fight so desperately hard not to use my magic. With my magic, I do not feel so helpless to the wants of others."

The old woman took Alainn's hand in her own gnarled claw and issued a sober warning. "I raised another who possessed the ability to do magic and you'll remember where that got her. She's not set foot near the castle in all these years and is forced to live out her years alone, but for the addled boy."

"He is now a man, Morag."

The aged old female stared at Alainn, though the filmy

white covering on her eyes prevented her from seeing much. "You keep away from her, caileag, for you'll be found guilty by association should anyone learn you've had contact with her."

Alainn looked up and gasped. The priest was standing in the doorway. He had come to speak with Morag. She hurried off to the kitchen to help Cook and his son with the meal preparations.

Chapter Nine

A LAINN LAY IN her straw bed waiting to hear the old woman's breathing become slow. After spending fourteen years in the same bedchamber as the woman, she had come to know her sleeping habits. When satisfied that her sleep had deepened, Alainn got quietly out of bed. She had left her frock on so she would be ready to leave. Knowing how the dampness made Morag's bones ache, she placed another peat log on the small fire in the room and pulled the covers up over her narrow shoulders. She eased on her slippers and found her cloak in the darkness.

Their room was in the tower directly above the great hall. Alainn used to lie awake in the evenings and listen to the music drifting to her on occasions when the earl and his lady entertained nobility. She loved to hear the sound of the Irish harp and the fiddle, and she adored the beautiful voices of the entertainers.

Thankfully, there was no feast this night. Though the servant who kept the constant fire burning in the enormous room was always nearby, she was fortunate not to see him. She carried her herb basket, in case anyone questioned her reason for being about at night. With the basket over her right arm, a candle in the left, she carefully made her way down the many twisting steps, the few sconces casting dim shadows across the stairwell wall.

The guard at the castle doors glanced briefly at the basket in her hands and simply opened the door for her. He knew her habit of going to collect herbs that needed to be cut after dark. The guards at the drawbridge, however, were always more cautious of people's comings and goings. The older of the two questioned her. The younger seemed more intent in getting a look at her backside. She hoped her explanation of Morag's rheumatism, and the need for more herbs for an ointment and willow bark for a tea to ease the pain would convince them. The older seemed to believe her and was in the process of lowering the drawbridge when the younger said, smiling suggestively, that it might be wise for him to escort her to the garden since it was a long walk and a moonless night.

"No, I am certain you are needed here," Alainn said quickly. "And, the garden is within the village walls. I will be secure enough, thanks to the fine job you and all the captain's men do in keeping watch over the earl's domain."

The older man puffed out his chest at her compliment, but the younger, who couldn't keep his eyes from trailing up and down her body, pushed on. " 'Tis quiet this night. Phelim can keep watch here for a time, and there are the guards in the watchtowers, as well. I am certain I can take a

break from this post, for a time. What do you say, Phelim?"
He jabbed the older man with his elbow and winked at him
so blatantly, she wanted to tell him she was not daft, that she
knew well enough what he intended to do once they reached
the garden. The older had still to make up his mind on the
matter when they heard footsteps coming toward them.

"Good evening, Milord!" they both said as they straightened to attention. Alainn turned to see which O' Brien was
approaching. She had never before feared the chieftain but
after reading his thoughts that morning she hoped it wasn't
him. Killian had been so angry with her, this afternoon, she
was feeling less than eager to meet him, as well. She decided
she hoped it would be Rory, but when she saw the dark hair,
her breath drew in sharply. She had no desire to make
acquaintance with Riley O'Brien after this day's events. He
must have heard the young guard trying to make time with
her, for he opened with a response to him.

"You needn't worry about accompanying the Maiden
McCreary, John. I am headed out by way of the garden,
myself. I'll see her there safely."

"Oh, aye, sir, you do that then, sir." He looked at the
chieftain's son with a knowing smile, though he lowered his
head when Alainn glowered back at him.

There was nothing she could do about the arrangement.
She knew no one would question Riley O'Brien's motives,
even if they might be less than honorable. She grew more
nervous as they crossed the bridge and entered the darkened

grounds. He still had said nothing to her, so she remained silent, as well. When he stopped at the stone fence that lead to the garden and waited for her to go in, she hesitated.

"For all your brave talk this day, you actually fear me, don't you, Alainn McCreary?"

"Aye, I suppose I would be a fool not to fear you, given the circumstances."

"Well, I've not come to harm you, so you can put your hackles down."

"Why have you come?" she asked, stepping back a pace.

"Killian has sent me to escort you to the dolmen."

Alainn was surprised Riley knew of their intended meeting place. "Why did he not come himself?"

"Well, I expect he sent me in hopes that I would offer you the apology he feels you deserve."

"And, you do not believe I am entitled to an apology?"

He seemed less than pleased at her words, but she did not expect his next statement. "Aye, I should not have talked in such a way to you or about you. You angered me and I often say rash things when I am in temper."

They walked on past the small houses and shops of the village. Candlelight shone through the many small windows and the smell of peat burning in the fireplaces hung in the air. They passed Cook's house and she could hear the noisy commotion from the busy household. They walked in silence for a time, and she realized this was the most time she had ever spent alone with this O'Brien.

He had always been a sullen, serious boy, and, now, a proud and arrogant man. And, though he had enraged her to the point of a violent outburst, it was because of him that she did not find herself in the dungeon this night. She headed toward the lowest spot in the stone wall, where she would usually climb over to avoid seeing another guard at the gate.

"Would it not be simpler to enter by way of the gate?" Riley smirked, holding it open for her.

"Aye," she nodded feeling foolish and realizing how being of noble blood made some things much easier.

When they got to the large dolmen where she was to meet Killian, she found the silence growing awkward. She knew she must ask him what had been weighing on her mind. "Why did you lie to protect me today, Riley O'Brien?"

He was silent for so long, Alainn thought he would not respond at all. Then, he spoke softly. "I thought of how much you detest dark spaces, and I couldn't see you sent to the dungeon."

"And, how is it you know of my dislike of such things?"

"I remember locking you in the dowry chest in my mother's room when we were young. Though you were sorely frightened and I knew it well enough, you didn't beg me to let you out. And you wouldn't give me the satisfaction of hearing you cry. When I finally opened the door and saw your pale, tear-stained cheeks, I felt as low as I ever have in my life."

"I didn't know you regretted it," she whispered.

"Aye, well, I did and I do, for though you may think little of me, I do not wish to see you despair."

"I have never disliked you, Riley O'Brien."

"Perhaps not, but you've had much more in common with Rory. And, you always seemed so happy when you were with Killian. I felt a bit out of place, as I found it difficult to speak with you. And, you were never unkind to me, even when I purposely locked you in that chest. I have not forgotten how you spurred me on in the lessons, either. I think, even Killian and Rory did not know how you wrote the stories in simpler, easier managed words so that I could understand them.

"And, when you wrote each chapter, purposely leaving it at a point where I needed to find out what happened next, you created a love of reading in me. For that, I am grateful." Alainn had never known Riley to sound so sensitive or sincere. "So, aye, I owe you an apology for today and a thank you for putting up with my childish pranks."

"Aye, I accept your apology and I must apologize myself for the scratch on your cheek. It was dreadfully unladylike. I should not have behaved in such a manner, though I'll not pretend to like how you treat women."

"No, I don't suppose you do, and I'll tell you that is not likely to change, for once a pattern has begun it is all the more difficult to end it."

The lantern flickered in the breeze and Alainn sat down

upon the smaller dolmen. She felt herself growing impatient. "I would have expected Killian to be here by now, what do you suppose is keeping him?"

"He had matters to attend to. And, maybe he's hopin' to cool down some before he speaks with you, for he was in a rare temper himself, today. You have a way of riling him. He has a talent for keeping the peace amongst our kin and our clan, but when it comes to you, his emotions overrule his clear head. I used to resent the time you spent with Rory and, most especially, with Killian."

"Aye, I felt your resentment toward me and was never certain how to make peace between you and me, Riley O'Brien."

"It was not that I resented you being around us, it was that I resented how you only had eyes for Killian." She tried to see the expression on his face, but the night was indeed dark and the flame from the candle only minimal. When she did not speak, he continued. "I am a proud man and I'm pleased to be an O'Brien, to be of nobility, but we are not so different, you and I, Alainn McCreary, for we both want what we cannot have and are surely destined to be less than happy for it. I think perhaps, it would be worth being a peasant, if it meant I might take you for my wife."

Chapter Ten

ALAINN FELT HER heart sink, in the knowledge that he was confessing his feelings for her and telling her she would never have a future with his cousin. She could think of nothing to say in response on either count. When they heard the footsteps drawing near, he cleared his throat and moved away from her. Killian entered the clearing carrying an enclosed candle. He seemed in a less than amiable mood, and Alainn felt sure she would feel the brunt of his ire.

"You've said your piece, Riley?"

"Aye, sure I have, and then some, I'd wager."

"And, you know, Alainn, it is Riley who prevented you from being punished?"

"I do."

"Then, it is best you leave us, Riley, for Alainn and I have much to discuss and I expect some of it will not be entirely pleasant. I thank you for seeing her safe."

Riley tipped his hat as he left and she nodded her good-bye.

Killian placed his light on the large dolmen formation, glanced at her quickly, then, turned away. He seemed about to speak, then stopped himself and paced back and forth, until she found herself growing nervous.

"Killian, sit down and talk to me!"

"I'll sit when I'm damn good and ready, and if I get close to you before then, I might be inclined to whip you, so you shouldn't push the issue."

"You are not my father!"

"Thank the Lord for that, for if I was I'd be likely to be done with you, as well!"

Feeling the sting of his words, she hopped down from the dolmen and walked toward the gate. He ran after her and gently clasped her arm. "That was very cruel and spiteful of me. Forgive me for my unfeeling words."

"You are not my father, Killian," she said, turning away from him. "You have no business entertaining the notion of whipping me as punishment. I remember you threatened to beat me the very first day we spoke."

"Aye, and then I didn't have the strength. You can rest assured, today, I do." He led her back to the dolmen. She shook her head in frustration, as she took her seat, again, but waited silently.

Killian began pacing in front of her. "Do you have any inclination as to how close you came to being taken to the dungeon today?" he asked. "Or, worse yet, to being lashed before the imprisonment? I always thought you to be of superior intelligence, but do you not know that flyin' at Riley as furiously as you did today, could be construed as traitorous? You attacked the man in line to be chieftain!"

"He deserved to be—"

"Hush your tongue, woman. Until I have said what I've come here to say, you'll not speak a word!" His harsh tone made it clear he demanded her obedience. "What makes you believe you can give your opinion to anyone and everyone regardin' any subject? You know a woman should not speak her mind when in a group of men. It is not proper, nor accepted. It is one thing when it is only you and me, or even Rory, for he knows you well, but there are others who would see you hurt. The priest is one of these men and he has the power to make it happen.

"I have just come with a meeting with my uncle and the priest. I have had to speak in your defense. For now, there is to be no recourse for your actions, for I've tried to appeal to them. You've had no male dominance and have not been disciplined by a man as you should have." She bit her tongue so firmly she made it bleed, the metallic taste filling her mouth. "And, I am partially to blame for your belief you might speak freely, for I have always encouraged you to speak your mind when with me, but 'tis not welcomed by most men."

He stopped for a moment and Alainn thought he was finished with his harsh lecture, but apparently he had only begun. "You cannot chastise all men for the wrongdoing of some. Aye, I know well enough your opinions on how women are treated, and I'm not saying I don't agree with you, but it is the way of our society, and I don't see it changin' any time soon. We are taught, as men, we are superior and, to be strong and powerful men, we must dominate everyone around us, most especially women.

"You can be furious at the way Riley and the others talked today, and you have the right to be, for they should not have talked in such a manner with you present. I don't care for their disrespectin' you and I have told them as much, but you cannot judge men for being with women in a physical manner. It is the way of nature. Some men assume it is their right to take whatever they want, whether it is offered freely or no, be it a woman, a cow, or a sheep." She stiffened at the insult. "Now, maybe it is and maybe it isn't. I like to think some men are honorable enough to treat women with respect and decency.

"I was fortunate enough to have seen my father treat my mother as a treasured possession, but a possession, nonetheless. And, you might believe men of nobility and position simply take any woman they desire, but you seem unaware that women use their many wiles and attributes to catch the attention of those who might improve their lot in life. For, many a nobleman has taken a mistress for a lengthy time and improved her station because she shared his bed. There are husbands who offer their wives and daughters to us for payment when they cannot manage their rents, or to win favor with the earl and his family. You cannot flay all nobility because you disagree with the practice. The male desire to be with a woman is a force so great, I doubt that a woman could ever truly understand it."

"Therefore, you are telling me your animalistic needs are so feral, you have no more control of such urges than a stag in rut?"

He glowered at her nastily. "You needn't make this so entirely personal. I was speaking of men in general terms."

"Aye, well, you appeared to be most definitely in rut when I found you with the miller's daughter."

"And, you are neither my conscience nor my intended, so it should be of little concern to you!"

"And, was she payment for due rent?"

"No, it was by her own accord that she came to me, and it was not me who initiated the intimacy. Christ, Alainn, you seem aware that it is a woman's duty to remain virtuous, but you are apparently unaware that it is an unwritten law that a man be experienced. It is expected of men, whether they truly want it to begin with or not."

He finally stopped pacing and drew near to her. She squinted in the limited light to see if he still appeared as angry as he had been. His voice seemed less harsh. He did not sit beside her on the rock, as he had often done when they were younger, but he did lean against it.

"I know with your abilities you are sometimes able to know what has happened, but I'm not sure just how much you know. Did you know my uncles took us to a brothel when Rory and Riley were not yet ten and six, and I, not much older? They had decided it was time the O'Brien lads became men and were introduced to those types of dealings with women. Now, Riley seemed pleased enough, and, as I've told you, male desires are strong and being with a woman in that manner is much on the mind of young men, and all men, I suppose. But, it is one thing to think about it, to want it, but quite another to have it thrust upon you. Rory was as nervous as a cat about the whole event, and I can tell you it was not how I might have chosen it to be. It is true that women, and most especially women of common birth, have little say in how they are treated by men and have to submit to men even when they don't want to, but there are expectations put upon men, too, even men of noble birth.

"If I had truly been given the choice, I would have preferred to have had my first experience with a woman, on my wedding night. A woman of my choosing, not a whore who'd been with hundreds of men and was only with me because she was being paid for the service. And, then, after you've been with a woman, the need is almost greater, as you know what great pleasure it brings. 'Tis liken to basking in the sunshine when you're cold and damp and chilled to the bone. Once you know how the sensation feels, you'd not choose to live in a shadow."

She felt herself beginning to understand.

"And, Alainn, I know well enough the dread you feel in having your husband chosen for you, but in truth, noblemen often have no choice in who they take for a wife. You'll know there are arrangements already made for Rory and Riley to be wed to the McDonnel sisters from the north."

"Aye, I've heard it said," she whispered. "And, you Killian O'Brien, has your uncle found a suitable wife for you?"

"He has spoken on the topic a great deal, trying to come up with the best match to form allegiance with the greatest political benefits."

"So, you'll not be permitted to wed the miller's daughter?"

He grabbed her shoulders roughly and pulled her down from the rock to stand before him. "I've heard quite enough talk of the miller's daughter. It was only the one time and though it's sorry, I am, that you came upon us, I'll not apologize for being with her. Why do you keep bringing up the event and what concern is it of yours?"

The light from the lantern shone on their faces and she was compelled to look into his eyes and reveal her thoughts. "Because, I wanted it to be me!"

He let go of her as if she'd burned him and stepped back. "You should not make such rash declarations to a man!" he finally managed.

" 'Tis the truth. I have wanted you as long as I can remember. And, aye, I remember well enough the journey you made to the brothel. I knew of it partly because of my abilities as a seer, but it was confirmed by the way the three of you acted when you returned. Riley walked about acting the part of a strutting peacock, Rory appeared embarrassed to be near me, and you, Killian O'Brien, became distant to me. Even though we still talked and met here on occasion, you no longer confided in me or told me your thoughts. And, since then, you have slipped further and further away from me. I have hated your uncles for it, for all these years, for taking your innocence, for robbing you of a meaningful experience, and for changing how it is between you and me. But, it has not changed my feelings toward you. I want you still and it stings me to know you only care for me as a sister or a disobedient charge you must watch over."

"My God, Alainn, is that truly how you think I feel about you?" He took to pacing again and, this time, she clasped his well-formed arm.

"Tell me what it is you feel for me, then, Killian O'Brien!"

Chapter Eleven

"I THINK," KILLIAN began, "I could never find the correct words to tell you what I feel." He looked down at the soft hand still holding his arm. "At first, it was gratitude for your giving me reason to carry on. Then, it was friendship and protectiveness. Not what a brother or father might feel, but liken more to a husband or a betrothed. I never thought of you as I would have my sister, for, when I looked upon you even as a child, I saw your beauty. I watched you often, when you didn't see. I watched the sunlight glint upon your hair and it gladdened my heart to see the sparkle in your lovely eyes.

"When I grew to be a man and you were still a child, I thought myself perverse when you came to me in my dreams. Now that you are a woman, so clearly and evidently a woman, with your unsurpassed beauty and your womanly shape, I can't keep my thoughts from you for longer than five minutes. I did not distance myself from you because I wanted it, but because I wanted you."

"And why did you not take me? Why then have you never taken me?"

"You were ten and three, when I first considered actually doing something about my yearnings! That would not have been proper. And, I would not have seen you hurt. If I were to be with you in that manner, even now, I could not simply walk away from you, or discard you, as you put it this afternoon when you were so displeased. Even today, seeing you in your enraged state, so passionate about what you believe in, though it angered me fiercely, it made me dwell upon how passionate you might be if we were to share a bed."

Alainn's heart thumped rapidly. Her blood began humming. She leaned closer, feeling the heat of his body, and looked up into his handsome face. "I am no longer ten and three," she murmured. "I want to know what it is to be with you. Show me how it is between a man and a woman. Make me yours, Killian O'Brien."

He tried to move away but caught the scent of her hair. He felt her body lean into his, her breasts against his chest, his loins growing firm. Her eyes widened, but she stayed close, wrapping her arms about his neck. So aroused and intoxicated by her was he that he took her in his arms. She angled her lips up to his and he claimed them as he had wanted to do for as long as he could remember.

The kiss was never gentle, not even from the onset. His hands traveled down her back to her hips, and he squeezed her to him as he pushed himself against her. He lifted her in his arms and sat her upon the rock behind them. His lips left hers to trail down her jaw and throat. She moaned softly. His hands found the laces of her dress and he hastily untied them. Reaching beneath the woolen material of her dress and the chemise beneath, he sought out the firm flesh of her breasts. They responded to his touch. His hands slid the garments over her shoulders, leaving her breasts uncovered, the cool night air and his continued touch causing her nipples to peak. When his mouth found their way to the hardened peaks, she gasped aloud and, clasping her hands tightly in his hair, pulled him closer still, ensuring he would not terminate his present actions. He moaned as she pushed herself into him and his already firm body strained against his trews.

His hand lifted the hem of her skirts and traced her leg from ankle to thigh. When he located that most private area between her thighs, her eyes grew wide with wonder and anticipation. She moved against him instinctively and his lips caught hers, once more, the kiss growing steadily more urgent until she moaned. He moved away from her and set her gently on her feet.

She watched him uncertainly. Removing his cloak, he placed it on the soft grass beside the dolmen, slid his sword from its scabbard to the ground nearby, picked her up as though she were a feather, and gently laid her upon his garment. He joined her and pulled her to him, kissing her again, this time softer, deeper, more slowly. Then, he stopped, and, for a moment, simply looked at her. His desire was great and mounting by the second. He fought the urge to simply ravage her and satisfy his lust and need by burying his face in her golden hair and inhaling the sweetness.

"My God, you are beautiful, Alainn," he said, his voice thick with arousal, "so incredibly beautiful. Even more lovely than I have imagined, and, believe me when I say, I have imagined you this way, often."

She untied his tunic fastenings and caressed his broad, muscular chest, gently touching the faded scar with her fingers, following it downwards. She unfastened his belt and traced to the end of the scar, just below his navel. She moved her hand lower still and dared to touch what lie beneath. He breathed in sharply, startled that she would be so bold. Though he'd not been with but a few virgin maidens, he recalled how shy and unresponsive they had been. This only proved to excite him further, knowing she wanted to touch him, so he unfastened his trews and assisted her in sliding them down his hips.

Her eyes met his, widening in awe of the proportions of the object beneath her touch. He could scarcely contain his need, as she caressed his manhood with an eagerness he delighted in. When he was at the edge of his control, he gently moved her hand and hastened to remove what remained of her garments. For a moment, he just gazed at her shapely form, savoring the complete beauty of her body. Then, he looked into her eyes so filled with passion and innocence. It was a precious combination, so rare and yet so fleeting. If they completed what he'd begun, the innocence would be gone, it would never be the same between them again. His mind and body waged a most vicious war with conscience and morals.

Seeing his hesitation, she pressed her body against his, saying, "Make love to me, Killian O'Brien. Make me your own. I have only ever wanted you. I ask for no promises, no words of love, no talk of forever. I am not a stupid woman, though I am foolish and fool-hearted to have fallen in love with you. I will not rue this night, no matter what tomorrow or the future brings."

He kissed her again, and she answered his kiss with equal fervor. He felt her tremble as he parted her thighs and found her womanly treasure, again. Alainn McCreary seemed prepared to accommodate his need.

However, knowing that she had not been raised by a mother and certain old Morag would not have informed her of matters of a physical nature between a man and a woman, he whispered softly in her ear, "Are you fearful, Alainn?"

"No, I trust you, Killian O'Brien. Have I reason to be fearful?"

"Well, I am not certain what you know of a woman's first time. I am bound to tell you there is certain to be discomfort."

"I have heard as much."

Her hand found his manhood, once more, and she seemed to be considering what he'd told her, assessing the magnitude of the object as she caressed it. "Is there to be discomfort throughout the entirety?"

"Only in the beginning," he said, his voice ragged with passion.

"I have wanted you to show me what is shared between a man and a woman, for a lengthy time. I have not been dissuaded by the knowledge there may be pain involved."

With gentleness and a patience he'd have thought himself incapable of, given his present aroused state, he took his time, touching her, caressing all of her till she moaned softly. He claimed her lips with his and her breathing quickened. Sensing her need, he positioned himself above her and slid himself in, moving slowly at first to minimize her discomfort.

She bit her lip and appeared in great torment. He was torn between his desire to continue and his concern for her. His eyes met hers with an unspoken question but she gasped, "I suffered a dagger in my chest and it did not kill me, Killian O'Brien. Sure, I'll survive this, just be swift about it and promise you'll make it worth my while."

"Aye, I can do that," he growled. That said, he thrust himself within her, and she screamed as loudly as when she'd been pierced with the dagger, then, cussed him fervently, making him smile. The light from the lantern illuminated her face and he watched her painful expression change to pleasure. The cussing changed to moans of pleasure. He looked into her eyes and she instinctively raised her hips to meet his thrusts. He felt a connection with her that he had never felt with any other woman. His own movements became more intense and he knew he would soon have no choice but to give in to his need. He felt the tiny shudder pass through her and she called out, "Killian!" in a voice filled with unhidden desire.

There was no mention of his clan name, for this moment was only theirs. He let himself slip over the edge to fulfillment.

⌘

THEY LAY TOGETHER afterward, her head on his chest, his arms encircling her in his love and protection. His breathing was still labored, his heart, still racing from their lovemaking. She shivered against the coolness of the night, and he tenderly covered her with his nearby tunic, leaning on his side to protect her from the cool breeze. He thought this was not the ideal location to take the virginity of a maiden, especially when the sweet lass beside him meant more to him than he cared to admit. She had been such an intricate part of his life, and, now, he thought he couldn't bear to be parted from her. He watched her smile as he looked down at her.

"You're not regretful, then, Lainna?"

"I've no regrets, Killian O'Bri—"

"Just Killian," he interrupted. "From now forward, you must call me Killian, for I think we've established that we're most familiar with each other." She snuggled deeper into his arms.

"Aye, when we are alone, when it is only the two of us as it is now, it shall be so."

He glanced toward the eastern sky, whose rose-colored hues would soon be accompanied by the morning sun. Lamenting the knowledge he must return her to the castle before the bustle of the day began and they were found together, he prayed that soon there would come a time when they could fall asleep in one another's arms.

Chapter Twelve

KILLIAN STOOD AT the garden gate, gazing into the castle. He could just see her profile through the arched window and his breath was taken away by her beauty. Her hair was tied back, but tresses spilled down her back from beneath her cap. Her plain grey dress was loose and shapeless, yet her body moved enchantingly. Her eyes sparkled and her full sensuous lips curved as she laughed easily at something Cookson must have said to her.

If he'd thought his need for her was great when he only imagined what it would be to make love to her, it was increased tenfold after he'd actually done so, now that he knew how her hair looked when untied, how it hung to her waist and shone with radiance, how it felt to have her locks caressing his bare chest. And, though he'd always thought her eyes an indescribably beautiful shade of blue, he had not seen them staring intently into his own, filled with unbridled passion. When he'd envisioned what it might be to disrobe her, to drink in her smooth white skin, it was nothing to having actually done so. Her perfect complexion was not limited to her lovely face. Her entire form was creamy and flawless.

He felt himself becoming aroused. What treasures lay beneath that dress! She had a small frame, but her hips were well formed and well rounded. Her breasts were firm and ample, fitting perfectly in his cupped hands. What it was to have his mouth upon them, to hear her soft sounds of pleasure.

Nearly six weeks has passed since the first time they'd been together. Four times more they had managed to steal away, to make love slowly and completely. Once, they had coupled hastily in a castle alcove. It had been no less memorable. He'd kissed her neck and touched her nipples through the fabric of her garments. They had hardened beneath his fingers. He had turned her away from him, raised her skirts, and entered her from behind. She had screamed out at the sudden and swift penetration, and he had tenderly whispered in her ear until their mutual desire had been abated.

She turned and saw him through the window, watching and admiring her. She laughed. Her shining blue eyes were filled with a new brightness and excitement that made his heart stir. She beckoned him inside.

Killian had often entered the kitchen as a young lad. Spending time in the wonderfully aromatic and bustling place had been commonplace, at one time. As a man, he had only been there a handful of times. It was Cook's domain and he would have welcomed Killian at any time, but Cook's immediate superior was the steward. The steward, though seemingly loyal to the O'Brien, and known for his efficiency in running much of the castle's daily activities, had two most untrustworthy sons.

Richard McGilvary, the youngest son, whom Alainn feared, was not only unpleasant but unpredictable. Alainn had told Killian of the horrid experience with the dog. He knew, firsthand, it was not only animals that were the brunt of his cruelty. He remembered well the many times, while out hunting, the despicable young man had purposely wounded the stags to watch them suffer before ending their lives. Richard had always insisted it was because of his bent and afflicted arm, that he simply could not be as accurate as he would like. But, Killian had also found him in the act of abusing a woman.

Now, as Alainn had said, there was many a man who simply took a woman when he wanted her, whether against her wishes or not. The day that he happened upon Richard McGilvary disturbed him, even to this day.

It had been far past the castle and the village. He had been out riding and had heard screams coming from the thicket. When he'd gone to investigate, he'd found a woman in great duress. Not only had she been beaten, but a knife had been used to wound her, as well. She was crying and pleading for her attacker to stop, but he continued to rape and abuse her violently, a look of twisted satisfaction upon his face. It was Richard McGilvary. Killian had beaten him, beaten him as thoroughly as he could without killing him.

The young man had spent more than a month in the dungeon.

Killian had implored his uncle to have Richard hanged for his crime, but his uncle was most hesitant to issue punishment by death to his loyal and valued assistant's son. When the young man had been released, he was ordered to stay clear of women. The steward, though greatly ashamed of his son, had taken a great dislike to Killian since then. And, after the day when Alainn had come so close to visiting the dungeon herself because of McGilvary's comments to the priest, Killian had blackened the trouble-maker's eyes once more.

Seeing his serious expression, Alainn wiped her hands on her apron and ran through the door into the courtyard. "Killian," she touched his arm, "are you well? You appear troubled."

"No, I am well enough, Alainn," he said, smiling broadly to confirm his words. He wanted to pull her to him, longed to kiss her, a deep and passionate kiss. He hadn't thought it would be so difficult to keep up the appearance that they were only friends. It was fortunate they had always been friends, for no one seemed to question when they spent time together, and, if anyone suspected they were more than friends, he guessed they might have thought them to be so for some time. But, now, as she stood so close to him and he could smell her scent and nearly taste her lips, he had to fight the urge to kiss her.

"I know you, and something had you vexed."

"Can you not simply read my mind, then, Lainna?" he murmured, daring to take a step toward her.

"I am never truly able to read your mind, Killian. And, as of late, I find my mind more than a little filled with distraction, and 'tis not your mind that has me so preoccupied."

She glanced around the courtyard and stepped behind the concealment of the kitchen gate. She playfully grabbed his hand and pulled him toward her where they shared a hasty kiss. He moved from her but remained looking longingly into her eyes.

"Alainn, have you finished with the broth?" demanded a stern voice behind them. They jumped apart and turned. It was the cook. The usually cheerful man wore a scowl upon his face.

"Aye, 'tis seasoned well," answered Alainn, her cheeks burning red, "and Cookson is adding the venison."

"Milord." Cook stared disapprovingly at Killian and bowed as he returned to his kitchen.

"I must go back within, Killian. With the celebrations fast approaching, every free hand is needed in the preparation. Have you seen the crowds of people who have come from far and wide? Of course there are the lords and ladies who will attend the event, but have you seen the many vendors and entertainers who have arrived? And, the celebrations are still weeks away. There is even a minstrel who is said to have performed for the English King Henry VIII!

"And, this morning, I spoke with a giant of a man. A man with black skin, from Africa. He was upon a slave ship bound for the Americas when he was shipwrecked. He was apparently the only survivor and has the strangest markings on his skin. And, he talks in such an odd manner. He took one look at me this morning and he told me I was a seer, a maker of white magic, he called me!" She bubbled with enthusiasm and excitement, and Killian smiled at her happy mood.

"Aye, it promises to be a grand celebration." He immediately regretted his words for he knew she would not be in attendance. She had never pushed to attend such celebrations, but, now, he wanted her by his side. He wanted to present her as his lady, to have her seated beside him, to show the world what a rare jewel he had in Alainn McCreary.

"I have never seen so much food or so many lavish dishes being prepared, and Cook has listed the dishes to be served during the feasts. There are to be hams, mutton, beef, and fowl, as well as the wild venison. Cook will send Cookson to the seaport next week to retrieve fish and seafood, and that's only the meats. There are to be breads and pastries, and cakes the like I've never seen before, and sweets in great quantity. 'Tis unfortunate the summer vegetables are not yet mature, for we have only the ones left from our fall harvest, and, with the cool, wet winter we had this year, 'tis difficult to preserve them. But, they are still adequate, and Cook has such a talent for making the stews and soups taste so tantalizing. The herbs wintered well, so they are a savory addition, to be sure."

He listened to her jabber on and found himself filled with contentedness. Her enthusiasm delighted him and he felt a stirring of emotion within his heart.

She stopped to take a breath. "You find me amusing, I suppose, to be babbling on about such simple topics as food and entertainers when you are much accustomed to such things."

"No, not amusing, my sweet Lainna. I find you delightful. And, aye, this is an unusually grand occasion, I suppose, to celebrate Rory and Riley turning one and twenty, and becoming of age. It is fitting. My uncle Hugh says this is the grandest occasion since my uncle Sean became of age and that was nearly ten and eight years ago." It would also be the official announcement of the twins' forthcoming marriage, but he knew that was a subject Alainn did not care for, so he left out that detail. His eyes must have depicted more, for she stepped closer to him again.

"You have come to tell me something. 'Twas not only to steal a kiss."

"Aye, my uncle has decided I am to go with Rory, Riley, and my uncle Sean to meet the coach that brings the guests from the north, the McDonnels of Glynn. He thought it a sign of good will to meet them and escort them here. They will have traveled far and, with the tension between clans and the English often at large, he thought it couldn't hurt to have extra security."

"Could he not simply send the captain and a portion of his guards?"

"Aye, well, he's sending some guards, as well, but he wants the O'Briens to offer them a warm welcome. And, bein' that Rory and Riley's future wives will be there, I suspect he'll want it known they're anxious to greet them."

"And, why is he sending you, Killian?"

"I think, he means to keep me out of trouble. He says I have appeared distracted these past weeks." He smiled the smile that always melted her heart.

"Does he suspect what has you so distracted? Does he know we have become close? Do you suppose that is why he is sending you off, so that we are to be separated?"

"No, I'm certain he doesn't. At least, I don't believe he does. He is a perceptive man, but, no, I think he doesn't know."

"When are you to leave, Killian?" she asked in an unhappy tone.

"We ride out at tomorrow's dawn."

"I shall miss you much, Killian, and I must warn you to be cautious, for I fear this peaceful time we have known is soon to end."

"Aye, there is much talk of the English invading our land. Thankfully, their king seems intent on focusing his attention on France, at the moment. But, 'tis surely only a matter of time, according to the latest rumors. There is much discussion as to which clans will side with the English and which will remain true to our want of Irish rule. The McDonnel's of Glynn have Scottish roots, and, in truth, their leader is a Scoto-Irish chieftain. Now, though Scots have fought the English as diligently as the Irish have, many are allying with the English. The whole of the country remains in uproar over the King of England's break with the Catholic Church.

"To suit himself and allow him to take his second wife, but that was a time ago, now, and they've already produced a girl-child. Apparently, he is displeased at her inability thus far to produce a male heir."

"So, you have heard of these events?"

"I keep my ears open and there is much discussion of it, especially with all the gossip that has arrived here with the visitors. Rumor has it, he searches for a way out of this marriage, as well!"

"Alainn!" Cook's voice called her from within.

"I must be off, Killian. Cook needs much help, and Morag will soon feel the need to come fetch me herself!" She turned to go, but he caught her arm before she could leave.

"Will you meet me by the garden gate, this night?"

"But, why not at the dolmen?"

"There are too many strangers about, many unsavory sorts. It is not safe for you to be about on your own, Alainn. You must promise me to be careful. And though, as you say, you can usually tell the good from the bad, that does you little benefit if you find yourself cornered by one or more of the wrongdoers."

"Aye, then, by the garden gate. I will see you this night."

Cook leaned his head out the window and directed his comment toward Killian this time. "Milord, I am wonderin' if you intend to allow Maiden McCreary to return to her duties, or do you foresee her keeping company with you for the remainder of the afternoon?"

Their eyes met and Killian thought it was in a challenge. He nodded respectfully to the older man.

"No, Cook, she's on her way." He reluctantly left her, greatly disappointed he could not kiss her good-bye.

Chapter Thirteen

"YOU'RE SURE TO get your heart broken, Alainn!" Cook's voice boomed throughout the small herb room Alainn shared with Morag. "You've a giant heart and filled with much love. I know it well, in how you are with my family and my wee babes, even with Morag. And, she's not so very easy to love."

"You needn't speak of me as though I'm not in the room with you, Seamus Kilkenny," snarled Morag. "I might be nearly deaf, but not entirely." Cook reasoned the old crone was the only one, other than his wife, who called him by name. As a child, she had cut him to the quick with that voice, and, even though he was a grown man of good health and sturdy girth, and she, nearly ancient and of broken health, she was still a feisty old woman and able to make him feel like a youngster.

"Well, you must set her straight on this, Morag. No good can come of her growing so close with the chieftain's nephew. I like him well enough, he's a good lad, and I've had a fondness for him since he was a boy, but he's a noble, and there's no debatin' that fact. She'll have her heart broken, mark my words!"

The old woman squinted her eyes to see the young girl who stood not two feet away from her. Her wrinkled face looked pinched with concern as she contemplated what should be said or done. "I have always said one day your friendship with the chieftain's kin will do you wrong," she simply stated.

"You needn't worry so much about me, neither of you," insisted Alainn. "I am a grown woman, and if my heart ends up broken, well I won't be the first or last maiden to end up with a broken heart."

"You'll not be so calm about it if it happens, caileag. And, I am not certain I'll be here to see you through that broken heart, for you know well enough my time is waning." The girl went to the woman and placed her head to her bosom, though the older woman had seldom shown affection toward the young girl.

"Don't speak of such things, Morag, for that will indeed break my heart."

"I have lived a long life, twice longer than most, I'd imagine. I am close to five and ninety. I know of no one in the castle or the village who has lived such a lengthy time." Alainn stifled a sob.

Standing silently to the side, Cook watched the two women and wiped a tear from his eye.

"But, before my time comes, I must speak with you of issues long kept silent. There is much you must learn before I can die in peace. But, not on this night, for I fear I am weary of mind and body. See me to my bed, will you, caileag?"

⌘

ALAINN STOOD AGAINST the stone gatepost and listened most intently to a man who had once been a sailor upon a ship that had traveled to the Americas. She found herself so intrigued by his stories of happenings aboard the ship and his descriptions of far off lands, that she did not notice Killian approach until he gently, but possessively, took her arm and steered her away.

"Killian, he was telling me of the Americas. I was interested in his words."

"Aye, and he was interested in beddin' you."

"Of course he wasn't!"

"Aye, he was. He was gawkin' at your arse, and he's lucky I didn't cuff him for it."

"Because a man looks at me, does not indicate he wants to bed me, Killian O'Brien!"

"Aye, it does, if a man is lookin' at your arse, he'll be thinkin' of takin' you to bed."

"Do you believe this because you are a man and you've wanted to bed every woman whose arse you've gazed upon?"

"You've much to learn about the desires of men, Alainn. As I have said before, they are not to be taken lightly."

When her chin rose a little higher, as it did when she was perturbed, his tone softened. "Besides, since I know just how lovely your wee arse is, I know well what thoughts the viewing of it evokes."

She did not respond, but clasped his hand as they walked together. He tensed at this and she pulled her hand away. "Does it shame you, Killian, to walk with me, for me to act toward you with familiarity in plain view of others?"

"Does it shame me? My God, no, Alainn! It fills me with a desire to shout to everyone that you are mine, that you are only mine. I am proud to walk beside you. My only concern is if the guards and villagers see us in this manner. I worry your good name and reputation will be tarnished."

"I am the daughter of a farrier who cannot keep away from the drink. I know what is said about him, and of me. I was raised without a mother or father, and most people think of Morag with fear, so I suppose I am pitied by many. I think my reputation and what people say about me is not so worthy of consideration."

"But, it is to me, Alainn, though I suppose you may not think so in that I continue to partake in immoral activities with you. I intended to be honorable toward you, Alainn, I assure you, I did not plan to act on my desires. Now that it has happened, I fear I cannot even consider being parted from you in that or any other manner."

"If it had not been you, I am certain it would have been another. Though men like virginal women, there are few who can retain that quality. I am only happy and relieved to have lost my virtue to a man I both love and desire. I'm not about expecting apologies for what we share. Nor do I want to terminate being together. Dwell not on what neither of us is capable of preventing."

With that, he regained possession of her hand and squeezed it tightly, knowing perfectly well what a rare woman he had in her. They walked together through the streets of the village, looking at the many merchants and vendors who had set out their wares for display. There were sweets and fruits, seafood and fish, trinkets and jewelry, many fiddlers playing, and much music in the streets. There was a festive feeling in the air, and they stopped for a time to watch a talented couple dancing a jig down the cobblestone street.

Beyond the village walls, many tents and temporary dwellings had been erected for the traveling vendors and entertainers. Though some entertainers were housed in the castle, most were found here. There was much rowdiness and storytelling, many campfires burned, the smell of smoke and the scent of whiskey and imported rum filled the air. They stopped to sample some of the food, and most everyone bowed to Killian. Those who did not know him by sight recognized the pin he wore as the O'Brien crest.

Killian watched Alainn. Nothing escaped her eyes, and he knew her mind made note of each detail so she would remember it always. As they passed by the last of the tables with displays, Killian noticed how taken she was by the baubles, but she simply walked past them without a word.

Always, when he'd been with women, in shops or markets, whether they'd been noblewomen, peasant maidens, or whores, they had wanted something. They would openly ask for something, he supposed, in exchange for their company or their favors. But, this woman who had known nothing of luxury or riches asked for nothing. She knew well enough he had the coin to purchase anything she might have spoken of, but she asked for nothing. It awed him and, because of it, he wanted to give her everything. He steered her back toward the table.

"Choose something," he said, "whatever you desire."

"I am not in need of material treasures. When would I have cause to wear any of these?" Her eyes danced across the many necklaces, pins, and earbobs, but she turned and began to walk away.

Killian let go of her hand and stared at the many colorful trinkets. His eyes caught two hair combs, shaped like butterflies and of a hue so like her eyes. He knew he must have them for her. He caught up to her and handed them to her.

"A gift for you, my sweet Lainna."

She took them carefully from him, then, stared up at him as though he'd just passed her the rarest and most exquisite of jewels. He watched her eyes fill up with tears. There had been few times in all the years he'd known her that he had seen her tears. She was always cautious not to allow herself to cry in the presence of anyone. He felt his heart ache.

"Aye, well, I'll return them if they're not to your likin'," he mumbled.

She clutched them tight to her chest and did not speak, though huge tears flowed down her cheeks. He took her in his arms and squeezed her with an intensity that made her gasp.

"No more tears," he whispered as he wiped them from her cheeks and placed gentle kisses upon her lips. He removed the worn woolen cap from her head and untied the hair she wore bound behind her neck. She passed him the combs and he placed them in her hair just above her ears.

"They are nearly as lovely a shade of blue as your eyes, but only nearly. They are turquoise from a land south of the Americas."

"I shall treasure them always and never be parted from them."

"One day, you will have gowns and jewels to match. You shall wear—" She placed her fingers to his lips.

"No talk of one day. No promises."

Chapter Fourteen

H E WOULD HAVE promised her the world. She possessed an understanding of the reality of their situation that he was less willing to accept. They walked in silence for a time, though he held her hand as tightly as though she might be pulled from his side at any moment. To dispel the quiet, he told her of a fair his father had taken him to when he was a child and they had visited England and Scotland.

"I read in books of these lands," she said, "and imagined how wonderful it would be to actually see those places. I have not even been so far as the extent of the chieftain's lands. Because I am able to ride a horse, I suspect I've gone much further than many who live here. Cook's daughter, Molly, has not been past the village gates, though, Cook is very protective of her and she isn't allowed out of his or his wife's sight. But, I am babbling on again, tell me of the fair and the purpose of your father's visit to England."

"Aye, it was when I was only ten years of age. My father was a nobleman of considerable wealth and influence and he was called to take audience with the king, Henry VIII, when he first took power."

"And, was it unbelievably grand, the Tudor king's castle?"

"Aye, it was large. My brother, Cian, and I found ourselves lost and had to ask directions back to the waiting area. There were many guards and a great lot of people coming and going. In truth, I found it all rather boring. And, Scotland was rugged with high mountains. It was much colder than here in Ireland."

"What manner of ship did you take for your journey?"

" 'Twas a swift galley powered by sail, though, there were many powered by strong men manning oars, as well."

"And, you've been to France, as well. I remember when your uncle attended the French Court and took you and his lads with him."

"Aye, that was two years previous."

"And, is it true what they say about French women?"

"And, what do they say about French women?" His eyebrow rose in inquiry.

"That French women are the most beautiful women in the entire world, and the most easily convinced to share a man's bed."

"Well, I've not seen women from all around the world, so I couldn't judge for certain."

"But, they are quite lovely?" she teased.

"Aye, they're pretty women. Many have curly dark hair and large brown eyes."

"Like a wolfhound, then," she remarked cattily. He laughed heartily, and she smiled despite her obvious jealousy.

"And, in regards to the other?"

"I've not been with so many women as you seem to believe, Alainn."

"However many women the count, 'tis that many I feel great jealousy toward!"

They had reached the fork in the path that would take them to the dolmen and she started down it. He called after her, "I've a surprise for you, Alainn. Come this way with me."

She followed him without question as they headed down the opposite path. They walked in the light of the full moon, talking occasionally, but often sharing a comfortable silence. He noticed how lovely her hair looked in moonlight. Up to this moment, he'd always thought it was most beautiful when the sunlight caught the many rich tones. When she was a child, it had been a paler shade, liken to a wheat crop in full ripe. But, as she'd grown older, it had darkened to a rich gold with the odd thread of pale gold entwined in it. It still had that silken, lustrous quality, and he was mesmerized by the way the moonlight danced and shimmered against her soft locks. She did not have curls, though she'd told him once she had sinned for she'd greatly longed for Molly's many curls, but many soft waves. When damp from the mist or the rain, it curled softly around her cheeks and forehead and the nape of her neck. And now, he recalled, after their lovemaking, when her skin glistened from the heat of their passion, it curled about her face even more appealingly.

When they had walked for a considerable time over the rolling hills, now damp with the nighttime dew, they turned toward the nearby lake. Her face lit up with excitement.

"We are off to the round tower!"

"Aye, I remember how you used to like to go there when you were younger. Though we were always warned to stay away from it, we never did, until Rory nearly fell to his death from the tower window. You prevented that as surely as if you'd pulled him back from the edge yourself."

"Aye, I saw the vision clear enough and it filled me with such cold dread, I could only whisper to you, and I thank the Lord you listened to me."

"I may not have listened or believed you if I hadn't seen you move the water in the basin that first day when you came to my room."

"But, that vision I had of your father, has never been proven true. Why would you have faith in my abilities after that?"

"Because we have not found him does not prove he is not alive."

"You have a strong faith, Killian."

"I do when it is something I am passionate about. And, I have a strong faith in you, for 'tis you who saved Rory that day. No one could have known about the loose stone by the ledge if you hadn't foreseen it. I shall never forget the look on your face when you spoke the words. You looked as pale as a spirit, and as though you might lose your breakfast where you stood."

"Sure, 'tis a terrible thing to see someone you care for die before your eyes as surely as if it really was happening."

"I suppose having the gift of sight is no kindness to the one who bears it."

"Aye, though I am thankful for the warnings and the ability to sometimes save those dear to me, 'tis not a gift I would have chosen to be blessed or cursed with."

"Well, there have been perhaps a dozen other accidents you have prevented, none so dire as Rory's fall might have been, but I would wager you've saved many a broken bone or other painful result. And of the other magic, the ability to see spirits, do you retain that, as well?"

"Aye, but I have mostly attempted to quiet whatever powers I have, for Morag tells me the more I use them, the stronger they will become, like a practiced craft. She says the more powerful I become, the more likely I am to win disfavor with the priest. I am most grateful to be able to speak of this with you, Killian. I believe Rory and Riley suspect some of what I am able to do. And, Morag, of course, knows of it and speaks of it with me when we are alone. But, you simply accept it."

Her tone grew so filled with sadness when she spoke of Morag, he stopped where they stood and looked deeply into her eyes. "What has you so melancholy, Lainna?"

"Morag is soon to die."

"Aye, well, sure it's to be expected, she's very old."

"Aye, she's lived a long life, but I know she will die very soon, perhaps in mere days."

"You know when a person is to die? By what manner does this information come to you?"

"It is not the same as when I am overcome with a vision to warn of impending danger or death for then I become sick at my stomach or deathly frightened. But, I know just the same. Their aura wanes. And, Morag's aura fades by the day. It is barely a soft glow about her now."

"I know you will miss the woman, and her leaving will pain you."

"Aye," was all she said as they walked. Then, she added, "The Glade Witch knows of my powers, as well."

"Do you still go to visit her and her son, Alainn?"

"On occasion." He gave her a look of deep concern. "I know, Killian, how you have always tried to dissuade me of so doing. And, for all my attempts to encourage you to go with me, you would not."

"I've truly no desire to see the woman who has cursed my family. I've always felt a bit hurt that you continue to seek her out knowing it was she who has caused so much pain for my kin."

"I could never condone what vexation she has placed upon your kin, for she has made so many suffer, but she has suffered, as well, Killian, and she has been sorely wronged by your grandfather, I suspect. Though she has never spoken of it to me, there is a pain and sadness that haunts her eyes. And, her child was always so eager to see me, for they see no one else, Killian. They live such a lonely existence. Even though you may feel it was a betrayal to you in my visiting them, I felt drawn to her and to that place."

"I worry about you when you go there. She is clearly evil and capable of much harm. And, the son, he must be a man, now. Is he dangerous do you think?"

"No, he is a giant of a man but as gentle as a lamb, and he takes such joy in small things. He adores animals and watching butterflies and lightning bugs."

"You have gone there at night? You have gone through the fairy glade at night and visited the Glade Witch at night?"

"And, you are fearful of both going through the fairy glade and seeing her, I realize that, Killian, but the fairy glade is a magical sight to behold at night. Like nothing else I have ever seen. You must come with me, one night."

"And, if the wicked fairies take me away?"

"They can only take humans who are truly evil or who have committed evil toward another, and you are a good man, and a kind man. They may be capable of small misdeeds toward you, but they could never take you away. That's absurd!"

"And, the rest of it is so completely believable in its entirety," he uttered with sarcasm.

"The witch would never harm you, if you were with me."

"How can you be so sure?"

"She tells me I am a more powerful witch than she is, that if I chose to use my powers I would be more powerful than I could ever imagine."

"How could she know this?"

"I am not certain, but she seems to know much of magic."

"Well, I still can't say I like the notion of you going to see her or going through the fairy glade. And, though I admit the thought of either of them sends shivers down my spine, if you are intent on doing so, especially at night, take me with you, for I'll only worry, if you don't."

She smiled warmly at him, and seemed most pleased. "I may not have journeyed to other lands, but a trip through the fairy glade is a journey few others have taken, and fewer still have spoken of. I will look forward to taking you with me, Killian. You will see why I always feel the need to return."

He was not remotely certain he would ever share her sentiments.

Chapter Fifteen

T HEY REACHED THE round tower and climbed the winding stairway to the top. Alainn gasped aloud as they entered the uppermost room. There were a dozen large candles scattered about the large, nearly empty room. A fire blazed in the long hearth, making the room lovely and warm. Flames cast a romantic glow against the stone walls and floor. A bedsheet covered the window, preventing the wind from blowing out the candles. And, in the center of the room, there lay a large bed covered in plush bedclothes and large plump pillows.

Alainn walked toward the bed and touched it. It was a feather bed. "I've only ever slept on a straw bed in the corner of Morag's room. This is so grand, Killian. How did you manage it?"

"I've my ways, and I've been planning it for a time, since the first night we were together and I felt ashamed to have bedded you upon the ground. You should be bedded properly, as the lady you are."

" 'Tis truly lovely." She felt tears brimming in her eyes, again.

"Enough tears, Lainna McCreary, or you'll make me think twice about doing things I thought would please you."

"I am well pleased, Killian. And I shall be forever grateful." She touched her hand to the combs in her hair. There was an underlying finality in her voice, as though she believed this might be the last time they would be together in this way.

He closed the distance and wrapped his arms around her as if he'd never let go. She buried her face in his chest and he kissed the top of her head. "I've brought wine," he murmured. He moved from her to present her a jug of wine and two goblets. Her sensuous lips curved upwards with pleasure as he poured her glass. She lifted the sweet liquid to her lips, then, quickly pulled it away.

" 'Tis mead wine, Killian! Sweet honey wine! Is it not ill luck to drink it when we are not wed? 'Tis not our wedding night." His face wore a look of yearning. "And, you've no need to increase your virility. I think fertility is not something we should be hoping for!"

" 'Tis only superstitious nonsense not to be considered truth."

"Like fairies and witches, and the like," she quipped.

He nodded his head and took her glass from her, dumping the contents of both goblets out the window. "I've brought whiskey, as well," he added and retrieved another jug.

⌘

KILLIAN LAY BESIDE her. It was the first time he had ever watched her sleep. She looked angelic, her cheeks, a soft pink from their recent lovemaking. Her long golden hair lay splayed across the pillows, tangled from their passion, yet sensual and alluring, He touched his hand to the lovely tresses. Her unusual blue eyes dominated her appearance for they always shone brightly and were filled with such vitality. Now, watching her sleep, he could take in all of her without being drawn into her eyes.

Her lips were curved in the slightest of smiles, and she looked peaceful and happy. His eyes continued downward to her perfectly formed breasts with their lovely curves and rose colored peaks, and the thin white line just about her right nipple. He had been jesting when he'd said she'd nearly lost it, but, it was not a jesting matter, for it would have been extremely painful and a terrible loss of something so beautiful. He softly traced the tiny scar and she emitted a contented sound, almost like the purr of a kitten.

Alainn had become a skillful lover in the short time they'd been intimate. She knew exactly what to do to ignite his untamable passion and unparalleled pleasure. Her wanting to please him was arousing in and of itself, but she also wanted to be pleased. She was not typical of maidens who had only participated in such activities for a short time. She thrilled to his touch and her desire seemed to be as great as his.

He noted the amulet she wore around her neck. He had

seen the thin leather strap it hung from many times, but he hadn't actually looked at the adornment itself, until now. She told him she'd had the amulet since she was a child, that it had been her mother's. The symbol on it looked similar to the pagan symbols he'd once seen in a book his aunt kept in her bedchamber. When they were younger, they often sought out the many books his aunt had procured though the years.

This symbol appeared to be a triquetra, a three-sided symbol used in druid mythology. It seemed unlikely that Alainn's mother would have employed druid beliefs, knowing that the farrier was a Christian. However, most would not believe his aunt Siobhan had once been a druid priestess before she married. The O'Briens had a devout Catholic faith, which often opposed the druid religion. His aunt did not practice her beliefs openly, but she did still partake in her reading and in observing the four holidays of Gaelic druids. His uncle may not have agreed with it, but he did not prevent her from her beliefs when she kept them to herself.

Alainn sighed softly in her sleep and nestled closer to him. He wrapped his arms about her more tightly and she awoke, staring up at him with a contented smile.

"Have I slept for a long while? Is it time to be going back to the castle?"

"No, sleep longer if you like, I'll wake you when it is time to leave."

"No, you leave on the morrow and I shouldn't be sleeping away what time we have left together."

"And what else might you be wantin' to do?" His eyebrow rose suggestively.

"Would you be capable of it?"

"Are you insulting my virility and insinuating I should have drank the mead wine?" he jested.

"No, not at all, 'tis only that it's been twice already this night, and by the amount of men who come to purchase herbs to enhance their abilities, I wasn't certain how often—" she stopped clearly uncertain how to phrase the delicate question.

"Well, Alainn, it is no herb that has made me so entirely insatiable, 'tis just being with you."

They were quiet for a time and Alainn closed her eyes, again, drifting off. She looked peaceful, in his arms, sharing his bed. He wanted her to stay there for all eternity.

"My plight is greater, Alainn," he said, speaking the words of the game of so many years ago.

She opened her azure eyes and beamed at him. "And why is your plight greater, Killian?"

"Because, you are so content, and I am not."

Her brows knit in distress. "You are discontent with me, with how it is between us? You must tell me what it is I must do to please you."

"I am most content with how it is with you and me, together, with all we share." He traced a finger on her brow to soothe it. "But, I want more, Alainn. I want to be with you always, not simply hidden away somewhere. I want to openly care for you."

" 'Tis not possible, Killian!" She sat up, pulling from his clasp. "You are destined for great things, things not achievable if you were to openly declare any intentions toward me. When it is time for you to leave, to take over the chieftainship of your father's land, then you must."

"It's not that I don't want to be chieftain, and my uncle tells me the clans still desire me over my mother's cousin, but it is not so important to me, as it once was. In truth, I should have gone to my father's land by now. I am of age. I think, I hesitate to leave for I am most certain whatever I find there will not be worth as much as what I would be losing here."

"But, you always told me of your desire to go there. I know you miss it still. When we were younger and I would ask you to describe your perfect day, the way you would live that day if it was your last day on this earth, your answer was always the same. I would make up irrational, impossible plans of how to spend my last day. Aboard a ship, or flying with the fairies, or some other childish magical dream. But, you never swayed from what you wanted. You were so intent on what your purpose would be. I remember it nearly word for word."

"Recite it for me then, my Lainna."

She smiled a warm, soft smile, and her eyes filled with light.

"YOU WOULD WAKEN in your bedchamber with your lady beside you, your children down the corridor. Through a window, you would look out upon the mist-covered lake to the north and hear the sea birds, for your castle was near the sea. You would look out on your land and be content. You'd hear the ocean waves hitting the shore, since you have missed that every day since you've been parted from the home of your youth.

"Your day would consist of soldiering and discussing battle strategies, and playing with your children. You would be respected by your men and kin, revered by your enemies, and loved by your family, most especially, your wife. You would live in peace and be thought of as a great chieftain.

"You would have the finest cooks prepare your meals, the most loyal servants whom you would pay fairly for their duties. Your evenings would be spent entirely with your family. And, when the sun set upon your perfect day and on your life, you would be in your bed, again, with your beautiful wife, who, throughout the entirety of your marriage, never tired of spending every night in activities shared by a man and a woman. And, you would die content."

"Aye, I suppose I should not have confided that last bit to you when you were barely more than a child, but you always seemed older to me, somehow. I always felt as if nothing I said would cause you to judge me. And, sure, I might have been a bit naïve to think anything could ever be as perfect or as peaceful as that sounds. I think, I was remembering how it appeared to be for my father, and I always aspired to be like him. But, always, when I imagined that dream, it was you who was my lady, Alainn, even long before I was able to confide to you how dear you are to me. It was as I thought it should be. I could care for you no more if you were daughter to the grandest most important of all nobles or ladies. You are all I want, all I'll ever want."

"What we want is oft not a possibility," she sighed.

She turned her eyes away, but not before he saw the sadness in their depths. He kissed her brow. "Now it is your turn, Alainn. Tell me now, what your perfect day in your perfect world would be. Would you still be aboard a ship having an exciting adventure? Have you found a fairy in the glade who will take you flying?"

She forced a smile and grew quiet.

"Tell me, Alainn. What are your dreams?"

" 'Tis foolish to dream of what can never be."

"Appease me, Alainn. Tell me what you would see when you awake in the morning of your most treasured day."

Reluctantly, she began. "I would waken in my stone cottage, my husband beside me." Her breath caught in her throat. "He'd be handsome and strong and very kind to me. When I looked outside, I would see the beautiful green hills and the sheep dotting the hillsides, the stone walls, visible, as far as the eye could see. There would be a fine mist over the land, and, when the sun came out, there would be a lovely rainbow just over the farthest hill. There would be an Irish wolfhound but not outside or kept in a pen, there, indoors with us, free to have reign of the house. And, there'd be cats, too."

"Dogs and cats, in the house?" he asked with laughter in his voice.

"Oh, aye, I'd see to it! The dogs would guard and protect us, and the cats would hunt the vermin. They'd be lovely companions."

He rolled his eyes and looked less than convinced, but he urged her to continue.

"I would be donned in a blue dress, 'tis how I pictured it."

"Blue, 'tis a color you favor?"

With a huff of mild annoyance, she replied, "Well 'tis only I've never owned a dress of color, always only gray or brown. I've not minded, not really, for 'tis common for women of my station, but if it is my perfect day, aye, I'd wear blue."

"Aye, it'd be lovely with your eyes."

"My husband would spend the day working the fields and caring for the sheep."

"You'd marry a farmer, then?" he asked. "You have a yen for farmers?"

"Well, they tend to have gardens, which, of course, I would need for my herbs."

"Aye, of course," he teased.

"I'd spend my day tending the herbs and preparing the

meals, tidying our home, but I would delight in every minute, even the chores, because it would be our home. I'd have a vast library of books to read and a comfortable chair to rock in. And, I'd have a horse to ride, so that I might gallop across the countryside with my hair blowing freely in the breeze, sometimes alone, sometimes with my husband beside me. I would still offer herbal remedies to those in need and feel contented in knowing I was of importance in my own right.

"And when the day ended, the sunset would be beautiful, and brilliant and perfect, and when I went to bed, in my huge comfortable feather bed, my husband would hold me and kiss me, and make love to me. We would fall asleep in each other's arms, and I would dream of the fairy glade and the lightning bugs, and all things magical. And, I would be content."

"You've not mentioned children, Alainn. Sure, you'd want children in your perfect life, for I know how you adore children."

She hesitated. "Aye, of course I love children, and if it was a perfect day, entirely, then, there would be half a dozen babes and children. But, you see I have always thought of you being my husband in my perfectly imagined world, and, always, I suppose, the curse was in the back of my mind, which would not allow for children."

His deep green eyes filled with seriousness. "Have you ever spoken to the witch about the curse? You have seen her often through these years."

"Aye, but she avoids answering. I think, she is not as powerful as she once was. I don't sense her being powerful. I am not certain she can lift it any longer. I am not sure she ever had the ability to end it, for, it is said that a curse uttered in furious anger is difficult to reverse. In truth, sometimes it can only be ended with the conditions of the hex being met."

His serious expression held an undeniable dread. "And, that is only when my line has ended."

"Aye. Or, if her child is accepted as nobility."

"That seems entirely unlikely."

They remained silent for a time, both deep in their own thoughts. Killian was startled when Alainn leapt out of bed, a disturbed expression overtaking her now pallid face, and began to dress in haste. He went to her side and grabbed her arm.

"What is it, Alainn?"

" 'Tis the witch's son! He is in grave danger." She was shaking. "The witch means to kill him!"

Chapter Sixteen

"SHE WOULD KILL her own child? She must be even more nefarious than I imagined!"

Alainn tugged her frock over her head and flipped her hair over the garment. The waist-length locks were disheveled, but she made no attempt to tie them back.

"She cares deeply for her son, I know not what might have caused this event, but I do know I must get to them straightaway."

"I don't suppose, I can talk you out of this?"

"No!"

"Aye, I didn't suspect I could. Then, it would appear I'm to meet the witch this night, for I'll not allow you to go alone." Alainn turned and kissed him hard on the mouth.

They hurried down the many spiraled steps and entered into the night air. A loud, tortured sound assailed their ears.

"What manner of animal could make that sound?" Killian queried.

" 'Tis no animal. 'Tis the witch's son. I fear we will be too late."

He took her hand and they ran down the path toward

the road that led to the caverns where the witch lived.

"We must go through the glade, Killian. Even now, we are not likely to get there in time. But, if we go round, I know it will be too late."

She held tight to his hand and pulled toward the many bushes that surrounded the open glade. When they drew near the twisted, gnarled branches, he could see no way to get through the briars and brambles, for they appeared tightly closed. He had never dared approach this closely and had never wondered how one might enter the fairy glade.

She looked at his uncertain face and touched her hand to her amulet. It glowed under her touch. She uttered words in a language he did not recognize, and he grew certain he wanted no part of this magic. But, barely were the words spoken, when the thick thorny branches parted and an illuminated passageway opened before them.

"Can a human without magical powers truly enter, Alainn?"

"Aye, if you are with me, you may enter. Keep your eyes low and do not look toward the bushes, for 'tis realm of the Unseelie Court. 'Tis an evil place, a portal to hell, it is said, but you are quickly passed through if you've no evil qualities."

"And how is it you know I possess no evil qualities?"

"Killian, we've not time to debate it. You come with me now, or I go alone."

He crossed himself in the way of his Catholic upbringing

and held tighter to her hand. As they stepped through the portal, he heard a most unpleasant humming sound, as though a thousand bee swarms had entered the trees. A foul stench hung in the air and an unpleasant sickly feeling filled his stomach. His skin crawled and his ears felt as though they would explode with the pressure and intensity of the sound. Alainn pushed on, holding tight to his hand, and soon the unpleasantness passed, and he found himself feeling warm and peaceful, and contented.

"What the hell was that?" he dared whisper.

" 'Tis the manner in which they communicate, the evil fairies and the creatures that live within the realm."

"Have you ever seen them, Alainn?" he asked, his face tight with fear.

"Only once," she said softly, "and 'tis all I ever hope to."

The air now smelled fragrant and light, and the glow seemed angelic, not eerie. He thought he would like to spend an eternity here. Tiny sounds of laughter and music could be heard, and whispers, all around them. Tiny balls of lights landed upon Alainn. She gently touched each one. They passed into an open glade and he noticed how she walked slower.

"Why have you lessened your haste?" he asked.

"It disturbs them if we act distressed. They must never sense our displeasure, for it saddens them and they may feel compelled to enter the human world to right the wrongs that have made our hearts woeful. It may upset the balance. And, time is not the same here. I have been here and thought I'd spent an entire day, but when I left this realm, in reality, it has been only hours. Time seems to be much altered in the glade."

"Alainn, what language was that you spoke? How did you learn it?"

"It is an ancient language, one of the druids. I am not certain how I came to know it. The first time I neared the bramble bushes, it just came to me, as though it was part of a memory I retained from another time, or another life."

They slowly made their way toward the opposite side of the glade. As they approached the other side, small orbs drew nearer to Killian. One touched his face and he jumped.

"They are charged with a force, liken to lightening, but in a much smaller degree, of course. They trust you, Killian, or they would not dare to land near you. If you were evil, their touch would only burn and mark you, but it might kill them."

"How do you know all this, Alainn?"

"I have come here often, and I have learned some by simply observing. And, they have talked to me."

"These glowing orbs speak?" he asked in disbelief.

"Aye. I think you could not understand them, but 'tis not only they who speak to me. There are dozens of different fairies that live here. Not all come out at night. Not all at this time of the year. 'Tis to do with the moon and the elements, but also with the druid holidays, for between

Samhain and Beltane this entire glade is amass with fairies of every variety, every shape and size. 'Tis a wonder to see. You must come here with me, at Samhain—"

She turned her head away from him. He touched his hand to her cheek and felt warm tears. "What is it, Alainn?" The orbs floated to her and all seemed to touch her at once. She seemed unaffected by the surges of energy they caused. "What saddens you, Alainn?"

"We will not be together by Samhain. I sense it."

"What do you mean we won't be together?"

"We will be parted, Killian."

"Do you see a tragedy? Is one of us to die?"

"I cannot tell. I don't foresee peril, but it may be too distant to recognize, for often I am only alerted to danger immediately before it happens. Perhaps, it is only that you are to be gone to your home. That is sure to be it. You are to reclaim your father's title, as it should be." The orbs clung to her and, as her skin glowed at their touch, she smiled. "They wish to console me. Their magic is capable of healing the body and the soul."

When they reached the gnarled, thorny bushes, once more, Alainn, held out her hand and the branches parted.

"You needn't speak the druid language to be permitted to leave the fairy glade?"

"No, only to be allowed entrance, and my powers of magic are always stronger after I have been in the glade." Killian noticed the buzzing sound was not nearly as prevalent now. Alainn lifted her skirts and ran as quickly as she could on the uneven stony surface that led to the caverns. Killian kept pace behind her. She stepped into the largest and looked around but could locate no one. The sound they'd heard from the tower bellowed, once more, and they moved toward the noise.

When they came to a precarious ledge, Alainn drew near the edge and carefully peered over. The witch's son lay at the bottom, his body twisted in an unnatural manner. The witch was kneeling beside him, holding his hand and comforting him. Her eyes looked up, and they were filled with despair. Alainn started down the edge of the craggy cliff. Killian took hold of her arm and tried to stop her.

"Alainn, you must not attempt to get down there! You'll break your neck trying, and there is clearly nothing to be done for him! If she caused this, why does she sit with him and comfort him?"

"I don't know the answer to that, yet, and I doubt any-one could heal him, but I must go to him, to speak with him." He didn't release her arm, but, knowing there was no way to dissuade her, he assisted her.

The descent was slow. The loud, painful, nearly inhu-man sounds that came from the injured man were most unnerving. When they finally made it to the bottom, Alainn ran to the young man's side. She took his hand and he turned his eyes to her. They were filled with pain and fear. He tried to speak, but it was obvious it hurt him. He spoke her name in a garbled manner, almost unrecognizable as speech.

Killian observed the young man laying there. His head was unnaturally large, his face twisted and malformed. The protrusion on his back was immense, and his legs, even before this fall, must have been gravely ill-formed. Yet, as Alainn had once told him, even through his misfortune and his obvious pain, Killian could sense no malevolence in the nature of the giant of a man.

He stood back, certain that his presence would startle the young man and disturb the witch. He stared at the woman, the witch, who had cursed his family. Now, in her obvious grief, she did not appear to be an evil woman capable of inflicting such discord on his kin. Aside from her wild, dark hair and tattered clothes, she looked as normal as any other. He watched Alainn place her hand to the man's cheek. He took her hand and spoke two words Killian could understand.

"My friend."

"Aye, I am your friend, Finn." She spoke lowly to the other woman. "Have you nothing to ease the pain? No remedies?"

The woman's voice was low and melancholy as she responded. "No, I've few herbs available here."

"Then help me attempt to heal him. Together we might manage it."

"There will be no healing."

"But, we must try."

"Touch his head. Tell me what you see."

Alainn gently touched her hand to his head and closed her eyes. When she opened them again, her eyes revealed great sadness. "He must have been in a great deal of pain for some time," she whispered in a barely audible voice to the witch. "His time would have been near, even without the fall." She took his hand, once more, and smiled brightly at the malformed face of the man. "You must go to sleep now, Finn. You are weary, I know it. Shall I sing for you to make you sleep?"

He nodded as best he could manage, and Alainn softly sang to him a song Killian had often heard mothers sing to their babies. All the while, she softly rubbed his forehead and tried to dull his pain. The man had stopped the disturbing shouting. Now, he only moaned occasionally as Alainn continued to sing. The thought crossed Killian's mind that if it was his time to die, he'd consider himself blessed to have Alainn's soft touch on his head as he left this world, her angelic voice sending him off to the beyond.

The other woman held her son's hand, her eyes tightly closed. The raspy breathing of the injured man began to slow and, within minutes, it stopped entirely. Both women sat there, neither moving, and Killian was hesitant to disturb them. It was the witch who moved first. She slowly removed her hand from her son and stood. Killian went to Alainn, knelt beside her, and kissed her head. She turned to him, tears coursing down her cheeks. He gathered her in his arms and held her as she wept. When she was ready, she moved, her eyes relaying her gratitude for his comfort. The witch stood watching the exchange, a displeased look on her face.

"You would dare bring an O'Brien here?" she growled.

Chapter Seventeen

ALAINN SIGHED. "IN truth, he is surely no more eager to meet you than you him. And, I think Killian's being here is the least of what we must discuss. Could you not have chosen a manner less violent, less painful? If you felt compelled to end his suffering, did you have no method more effective?"

"Don't judge me, Alainn McCreary. I have listened to him cry each night for a month past. I knew he was not to be healed. I had no potion to relieve the pain, no poison quick and painless. This was to be quick. It was to be instant. It did not turn out as I had hoped," she said wearily. "How did you know of my intentions? Was it your powers that alerted you?"

"Aye, I had a vision. I saw you luring him to the edge of the rocks with the lightning bugs, his face was full of wonder as it always was. And, I saw you behind him, was certain you would push him."

"Well, as it turned out, he slipped over the ledge. His unsteady legs insured I would not have to do the actual deed."

"You know I would have brought you a potion to assist with the pain. You could have contacted me if you'd tried."

"You have been preoccupied, these past weeks. You have heard none of my summoning spells. And, I doubt you would have assisted in the ending of his life, for you still retain the goodness that keeps you from embracing your true power and potential. Now, I see the reason for your distraction and for your long absence from this place."

Killian, listening to the exchange and only understanding a portion of their words, felt spurred to respond. "Are you telling me you caused your son to fall from that precipice?"

She glared at him and he felt his skin prickle, his blood chill. Her eyes held a vaguely familiar quality. "I will not speak to an O'Brien."

"Aye, well you clearly spoke to my grandfather and cursed the lot of us in so doing!"

Alainn stood between the two. "He was very ill, Killian. He had an abnormality within his head. She did not push him. Aye, she may have lured him to the edge, but it was to end his suffering."

"So, you agree with what she's done?" He sounded horrified at the thought, his disgust evident on his face.

"Ah, the strong Catholic upbringing of the O'Briens has left you judging everyone as your grandfather did," sneered the witch.

" 'Tis not my upbringing that knows it is wrong to commit murder!"

"Perhaps, if you'd listened to his pain, heard his pleas to help him, you would reconsider, O'Brien. He has lived his life with ailments that made life difficult for him, and he never seemed affected by any of it. But, this illness that would have surely taken his life in mere weeks was different. It would have been cruel to allow it to continue, knowing it would only become worse."

"Aye, well, I can understand your reasons, but cannot condone it. 'Tis not for us to decide when to end a life."

"And, if he'd been a warrior in battle, had been run through with a blade with no hope of living, if he'd been a kin of yours, would you not have ended it for him, if he'd wanted it?"

Killian hesitated. "Aye, perhaps. I suppose, I could not say unless I was in that predicament."

"Aye, so you'd best not judge me, O'Brien," she snarled.

He did not answer, but went to the body of the large man, instead, and, with great effort, hauled him over his shoulder.

"What are you doing?" the witch demanded.

"I assume you would like your son taken to where you would have him laid to rest."

"You would do that for me?"

"No, not for you! I would do nothing for you, for I despise you and everything about you. I do it for my Alainn and for your son, for he did not wrong me, nor mine."

"Your Alainn! You dare to suggest she is yours? Aye, perhaps now, for a time, while it suits your needs, but when you wound her, when you scar her heart as only one of nobility is able, you will have me to contend with, O'Brien!"

"I would not hurt, Alainn! She is—"

"Enough, the two of you!" Alainn cried. "Do not speak of me as though I were not present, as though I am a child to be protected, or a possession to be bartered over! 'Tis not the time, or the place to debate my feelings or my future, for, in truth, neither of you have a say in what is to be."

Killian turned and walked to the cliff face, holding the body of the immense man. Alainn touched his arm, her ire dissipating as she spoke.

"I will attempt to assist you, Killian." She placed her hands upon his back and shoulders, and warmth and power surged through his muscles. It was reminiscent of when she had healed his wound, but, with no wound to heal, it served to make his burden much lighter. She removed her hands from his back, placed them to her temples, closing her eyes. The weight he carried upon his shoulder lessened even more. Alainn stayed in the same position until he had hauled the weight up the steep ascent and lifted the body over the top of the ledge. Then, she released the force that had been assisting him and began the climb herself.

The witch selected a spot to lay her child to rest and Killian located a tool suitable for the task. The ground was rocky and the task a difficult one. The entire time he labored so unfalteringly, the witch stood and stared at the man, a look of disbelief on her face. When the young man had been given a proper burial, the witch spoke, her words directed to Alainn.

"Your man's father was a good man, too. I acted hastily when I cursed the entire line. I was young and many great injustices had been done to me. I meant to punish the man who committed the crimes against me, but my rage and my magical powers were so strong, I lashed out at him in a way I hoped would ensure his suffering would have long term consequences. I do not regret cursing the man, for he was horrid and despicable. Would that I had the abilities to change the curse now, I would do it for you."

"You must find a way," she insisted. "There has to be a way! Have you not sought assistance from the fairies?"

"You forget, Alainn. I am no longer permitted within the glade, and 'tis only the bog fairies and the solitary fairies outside of the glade who will speak to me. I fear they will be of little help."

"What will you do now?" Alainn asked in a softer voice. "Will you stay here, now that your son has gone? There is little keeping you here."

"I will stay for a time, for I sense I will be needed here soon enough." Killian was startled to see the older woman smile at Alainn, and, then, it was though they took part in a conversation, yet uttered not a word.

ALAINN HAD ONLY been capable of hearing the witch's thoughts for the past year, though the witch had been able to read Alainn's mind since the first time they'd met. It was an unusual way to communicate, but it had been effective when discussing matters they had not wanted the witch's son to overhear. Now, the older woman seemed to want to discuss a matter without Killian listening.

Go back through the glade, she said into her mind, *and take your O'Brien with you, for he looks as though he is in need of a time in the glade. And, he has helped me this night, so perhaps you should take him to the spring, Alainn. You may not know it, but all things are magical in the glade, most especially the joining of a man and woman.*

She raised her eyebrows at the girl and a blush crossed Alainn's cheeks.

Killian looked suspiciously from one woman to the other.

Why would you want me to share a physical love with an O'Brien, when you know it could only end in heartache for me? And, why would you think it was a wise consideration when the result could be a child that would never be allowed to live because of your infernal curse?

But, you already share a physical love. That much is obvious! I see how he burns for you.

Alainn tried to keep her mind clear and cloud the other thoughts that had kept her so preoccupied as of late. Immediately, the witch sensed what she was doing.

So, you have learned to block your thoughts from me! I

*thought you would discover that power soon. What do you wish
to hide from me?*

Killian looked as if he would speak, so Alainn said aloud,
"I am sorry for your loss, Mara."

The other woman only nodded to her. As they turned to
leave she called out to Alainn. "How goes Morag?"

"She fades steadily. Her time is short."

"Tell her I think of her often."

"Aye, I'll do that."

Alainn waved to her as she and Killian walked off together.

"What just happened between the two of you?" he demanded, when they were out of hearing range of the witch.
"You are able to talk to her without speaking, aren't you?"

"Aye, for a time it has been possible."

"She said something that disturbed you. I know you,
Alainn. What has you so deep in thought?"

She was not eager to discuss this with Killian, so she
simply smiled at him. He looked weary, exhausted from the
strenuous tasks he'd completed. His shirt was stained from
the sweat of his labor. His hands were caked with dirt, and,
when she attempted to take his hand in her own, he winced.
She turned over his palms to see many blisters and dried
blood. She placed his dirt-covered hand to her lips and
hoped his discomfort was lessened some. Her powers had
been greatly drained with the exertion of making his ascent
up the cliff less difficult and she had been left with no reserve

to assist with the digging of the grave. She reasoned that a time in the glade would be a luxury they both could use, at the moment.

Chapter Eighteen

TRAVELING THROUGH THE bushes and into the fairy glade was not nearly as disturbing this time, though, Killian was uncertain whether it was because he knew what to expect or because he was dwelling on Alainn's silence. She had scarcely said two words since they'd left the witch. Perhaps, she was simply grieving for the sad and short life the witch's son had led. When the brightly colored orbs landed on her, Killian could hear a tiny fluttering sound, as though they were speaking, and they clung to her without leaving.

The moon shone brighter in the night sky. The entire glade was illuminated with a warm golden glow, and he took notice of streams and trees he hadn't seen before. Alainn steered him into a small wooded area. He stopped and gasped. A waterfall was suspended in mid-air. As if streaming from nowhere, it flowed into a large pond that bubbled like a spring. A low mist of heat hung over it. The night air felt warm against his face, and there was a faint scent emanating from the water. It was liken to lavender. Alainn still had not spoken, but she came to him and began untying the fastenings of his shirt. "I'm not certain we've time for this,

Alainn," he said. "I must ride out at dawn, and it surely approaches. I fear I must get some sleep, too, or I'm liable to fall off my horse on the long ride ahead of me. And, I'm not entirely sure I want to disrobe with all your wee friends, here watching."

Alainn whispered in their language and they obediently flitted away.

Only the sound of the waterfall and the bubbling water could be heard. "The water has healing qualities, Killian. Your tired and strained muscles will be much improved, and your damaged hands, as well. A swim in this spring is as beneficial as a lengthy sleep. It restores you in a remarkable way."

"Aye, then I'll take a wee swim, for it looks greatly appealing, but only if you'll join me, then."

"I could use a time in this water, as well. 'Tis truly a delightful experience. This is one of my favorite places within the glade."

He watched her remove her garments, mesmerized by the pale skin that now glowed in the moonlight. She met his gaze and smiled for the first time since they had left the witch. He stepped into the swirling water, shocked at the heat of it. As he slowly made his way deeper into the water, the warmth enveloped him and he thought he'd never felt anything quite so heavenly. Alainn smiled knowingly and immersed herself to the neck, closing her eyes as the water bubbled and churned around her.

Killian swam nearer and pulled her to him. He no longer felt fatigued but incredibly aroused. The water against their naked bodies was thick and sensual, and when their silken skin touched, there was an enhancement of their desires. They began caressing each other, the warm water stoking a fire deep within them. Their bodies moved rhythmically and their breathing became ragged. He grasped Alainn, lifted her up, and, standing tall, drove her down onto his manhood. So intense was the meeting of their bodies that she cried out his name. He took her mouth with his, their kisses hot and wet as the water around them, their motions swift and dizzying in the swirling pools that bathed them. They reached their crest together, crying out into the night, then, slowly, slipped into the water in a state of complete contentedness.

"Might we stay here forever, Lainna?" Killian murmured against her wet hair. "To live out our days, you and I, in peace. No one to interfere with our love. No reason to be concerned that we may be parted."

"Aye, it would be heavenly. But, you would tire of it, Killian. For, you'd be distanced from your cousins and your uncle, and all that you hold dear in your heart."

" 'Tis you who makes my heart sing, Alainn. I believe I could spend eternity with you here in this magical place."

"You'd miss the soldiering and the hunting, for the fairies do not take kindly to weapons in their realm. And, you would miss the contact of male companionship."

"Ah, but perhaps we'd have a son. Surely, the curse

couldn't touch us in this beautiful glade. If the witch cannot even enter, sure her spell cannot reach us here."

"And, I've Morag to think of, Killian. I must be with her when she passes, and there is the matter of your chieftainship to be considered."

She swam across the spring and dove beneath the waterfall. He joined her and, for the moment, they simply delighted in the water, the warmth, and their time together, splashing each other and acting as children. After a time, Alainn moved away to the shore and lay upon the bank.

"You've had enough of this glorious healing water, have you, Lainna?"

"Aye, my fingers are puckered from the length of time I've been in the spring."

He lifted his hands to look at his own and was startled to find the blisters had completely healed.

"I imagine your back and shoulders no longer ache," she said, smiling lazily.

He rolled his shoulders and back. The ache he'd felt across his shoulders was indeed gone. He chuckled at the realization of it. "How do you leave this place, when 'tis so calming and beautiful?" he asked, rolling his shoulders, again.

"Even with the fairies and the sprites and the like, it can be lonely here. And, though the evil fairies and the creatures of the Unseelie Court are not able to enter into the center of the glade, there are other dangers. There are portals that lead to other realms, to other times. Humans and witches alike have disappeared within, never to be heard of again."

"You may make a journey through time, by entering a portal in this glade? Have you attempted it, Alainn?"

"No, I've steered away from all the portals."

"That's not like you to pass up an opportunity to have an adventure."

"I was never certain if I would be capable of returning, and always the thought of being forever parted from you kept me grounded here in the glade."

"You said you had seen the beasts and creatures within the brambles. When was that?"

Alainn sat up and wrapped her arms around her legs. "It was the day I so nearly caused the death of Richard McGilvary. I wanted him dead, as sure I breathe, and I almost killed him with my powers. The sensation I felt, when that thought went through my head, caused me much grief so I went to the glade to relieve myself of the ill feelings. 'Twas, then, I saw the creatures. They are too hideous to dwell on for long. 'Tis why the witch can't enter, because she hexed your family. She committed an evil and, if she attempts to enter, she'll join the realm of the Unseelie Court. It is a growing realm of hellishness." She shivered, even in the heat.

"But, tell me, Alainn, how would a human enter the glade? You know the language that enables passage, and I've seen how your amulet glows when you draw near to the portal, but how might a human enter without benefit of magic?"

"The Unseelie Court opens to people or magical beings if they possess even a trace of evil. But, when it is opened, it often swallows them up, takes them into their realm. If the benevolent fairies venture out of the glade, as when the balance is disturbed, they leave an opening, a door to the glade that anyone might stumble upon. People can enter, but so can those in the Unseelie Court leave. Sure, we would not be alone entirely, even if we relished the thought of living here in peace."

Alainn lay back down upon the soft grass. It was a lovely type of grass, as soft as silk and warm to lie upon. She gazed up at the stars and listened to the sounds in the night, the water babbling and the soft breeze in the trees around them. Her eyes drifted shut.

⌘

SHE FELT HIS warmth beside her. He caressed her shoulder and touched his lips to her cheek. "You're no longer tired, then, Killian?" she asked, opening her eyes and smiling up at him. "You will make the ride without incident?"

"Aye, I feel entirely invigorated!" he growled playfully. "I feel as though I've just wakened from a lengthy nap. What power must exist in this water? But, you're sleepy again, Lainna. Does the water not have such an effect on you because you have magical powers?"

"No, I am well rested, now, just hesitant to move, for,

then it will be time to leave the glade, time for you to be on your journey. I despair at the knowledge we'll be parted for near a week."

His lips found hers and he kissed her deeply, then, he moved slowly, brushing them gently down her throat and over her breasts. She felt the familiar tingling within her and pondered how he could bring her desire to life so quickly, again. His lips continued downward across her abdomen and when they traveled further still to the fork of her legs, she gasped at the sensation of pleasure. Waves of erotic ecstasy pulsed through her and she arched her hips to his mouth as the ripples radiated through her body. When she thought she could bear the intensity of it no longer, he removed his lips, and she felt him penetrate her.

She looked into his eyes as she met his thrusts. Soon he capably lifted her so that she was atop him. She rode him with such wild abandonment that she was soon at the pinnacle, again. As she watched his magnificent form move with her, she sensed his release was soon to come. She heard him moan and it drove her over the edge, her world exploding into magical degrees. Still joined in intimacy, she leaned in to tenderly kiss him and he whispered in her ear, "I love you, Lainna. You will always be only mine. I'll see it so."

Chapter Nineteen

A S THEY MADE their way to the castle, the light of dawn had yet to appear, but it was approaching fast. The castle lay quiet, most of its residents still asleep. Cook would be in the kitchen along with many of his staff, busy preparing the immense breakfast required to feed the O'Briens, their kin, and their guests. Alainn's stomach grumbled a protest.

"Come break fast with me, Killian, for you must eat before you begin your journey. We may sit in the chamber off the kitchen. Let us have this time together before you are off."

"I think Cook will not be so pleased to have me in his kitchen, Alainn. He is much perturbed with me as of late."

"He's concerned you'll break my heart. He worries about me as he does his own children."

"He believes I have acted dishonorably toward you."

"Aye, well, I can set him straight on that count, if you like."

"And, how might you do that?"

"I'll admit I pursued you, that I threw myself at you."

"Why would he believe that?"

"Because, in truth, that is how it happened, and he knows I never speak lies." He looked at her clear blue eyes. She did speak the truth, sometimes to a fault, and he had never heard a lie fall from her lips. "Come with me, Killian. Sure, you must be hungry."

"Aye, we surely worked up a mighty appetite. I'll join you, then, and hope Cook does not toss me out on my ear. But, it must be quick, for I intend to meet with my uncle this morning before I set out," he said in a determined voice.

Cook stared at the girl as she entered the kitchen. Her hair was disheveled, her cheeks a bright pink, and radiance shone from her pretty blue eyes. She looked, indeed, like a young woman whom had just been well bedded and not objected to it. And, a few steps behind her, was the chieftain's nephew, the culprit who had surely deflowered the maiden. He'd suspected they'd become intimate, but seeing her in this manner, knowing they'd been out all night partaking in adulterous behavior, made him fume.

"Good morning to you, Cook," she beamed. He nodded curtly.

"You've been out all night then, have you?"

"Aye, it's been a most eventful night."

"Aye, I can tell by the look of ye, it's been eventful, but you needn't be so brass about it, Alainn. You're sure to be on the verge of spoilin' your reputation sorely. I thought you had more sense, lass!"

"Don't be cross with me, Cook. You know how I feel about Killian."

"Aye, but you well know how I feel about the entire situation. It will end badly!"

"The witch's son has died this night, Cook."

"The child has died? And, what was the cause? Was it his many maladies that took his life?"

"No, 'twas an accident, but aye, he had many ills. He would have surely died soon at any rate."

"Ah, so, Mara, the witch is alone now." The witch, once called Mara, had been a charge and an assistant to Morag and Cook knew her well. He glanced coolly at Killian, then, started at the state of his filthy clothes. "And, what have you been up to, to have managed to get yourself in such a state?"

"He prepared the grave for Finn, Cook, for Mara's son."

"Jesus, Mary, and Joseph, don't let the chieftain hear that or he'll have your hide, Killian O'Brien. For an O'Brien to have anything to do with her is surely a law to be strictly adhered to, and for you to aid her in any way, lad. You'll not win favors with your uncle over this, I assure you."

"Aye, well, I'm certain that won't be the only point of contention between my uncle and me in the foreseeable future."

Cook looked at the man standing beside Alainn and noticed how he gazed at her. Killian O'Brien was not only bedding this young woman, he was clearly and undisputedly in love with her. Hugh O'Brien would be gravely displeased, outraged, if he learned of their feelings for one another. And, by the determination on the young man's face, Cook was quite certain that revelation was soon to be declared. He thought he might like to be a fly on the wall to overhear that conversation. But, he was most certain that one or both of these young people was sure to be deeply hurt. The chieftain would find a way to keep them apart. He'd seen it before with Hugh's father. He had forced two young people desperately in love to be parted, and, now, history was surely to repeat itself.

"Alainn," he said, relenting, "get the two of you some plates, then, and be swift about it, for I assume the lad would like to find some clean clothes before he sets out on his journey. The guardsmen and the chieftain's sons are already in the banquet hall awaiting their meal."

"Aye, but are you certain the ham is not rancid, Cook?" Alainn asked, scrunching her nose. "It has a fetid odor about it and the mere scent of it has left me queasy."

Cook looked hard at Alainn, glared at Killian, then turned and cussed loudly under his breath.

"You needn't take offense, Cook. I didn't intend to insult your cooking—"

" 'Tis not insult I am feeling this moment, Alainn McCreary," he growled.

"You are acting most peculiar, Cook."

"Go, girl, and take your lad with you. Break your fast before he must leave you, and then get back here to the kitchen. There is much work to be done from now and until the celebrations."

"Aye, to be sure." Alainn concentrated on the Cook's red face and dared to read his thoughts. "Oh!" was all she said.

With his back to Killian, Cook hissed, "Have you told him of your condition?"

"No!" she hissed back. "There will be no disclosing this, not to him, not to anyone, Cook. I beg of you, keep this to yourself."

"For now, if it is what you desire, it will be as you wish."

"Thank you." She hastened to go get Killian his meal.

⌘

THEY SAT TOGETHER, in the tiny chamber off the kitchen. Killian ate heartily and Alainn fetched him a second plate. He glanced around the small room, looking at the vast array of vials filled with Alainn's potions. There was an acrid scent in the room, but it did not prove to abate his appetite. She sat upon Morag's stool and he, on the large wooden trunk filled with dried herbs and potions. They talked comfortably and Alainn felt strangely content, considering the precariousness of her situation.

"You've barely touched your meal, Alainn," Killian commented. "And, the ham is most definitely not rancid but entirely delicious. Between the healing water of the spring and this hardy meal, I will be sustained until we reach the Midway Inn. 'Tis halfway to where we will meet the visitors from Antrim."

"And, are there brothels near this inn?"

He raised his eyebrow. "Aye, as in any seaport, I suspect."

"You do not suspect, Killian, you know well enough as you've frequented them on more than one occasion!"

"And, you are jealous, Alainn, of my past indiscretions?"

"Aye, I am fiercely jealous. Would you not feel unkindly toward other men if I had been with others?"

"But, you haven't, Alainn. And, 'tis not the same for a man and a woman!"

"That may very well be, but, though I've asked for no promises from you, I will promise you one thing, if you bed another while you are bedding me, I will not take kindly to it and we will not share that intimacy again. Not ever. I swear that to you!"

He pushed his plate away from him and stood. "By, Christ, woman! You know how to rile me! Have I not told you how I feel for you? Can you truly think so little of me you would believe I would need to seek out a whore, when my loins ache only for you? You insult me, Alainn! Do you think me so entirely dishonorable?" She would not meet his eyes, and he went to her, lifted her off the stool. " 'Tis you I love, and you I desire. I swear on my mother's grave it shall only be you, from now on."

"I don't expect forever, Killian, but only for this time we have together."

"I must go, Alainn," he said, his annoyance clear on his face. "I suspect Rory and Riley will be near ready. I must find clean garments and see to it your father and the stable boys have my horse prepared for the journey."

"Sure, I'd like to accompany you, Killian," she said in a small voice. "If it were a possibility, I would dearly love to ride beside you, to the ocean. For, I have always longed to see and hear it as you make it sound so appealing when you speak of it with such fondness."

"Aye, and I would take you with me to the ocean and to wherever you desire, if it were a possibility." He turned to leave, but went to her again and gathered her to him. "I shall miss you so, Lainna," he said and kissed her tenderly.

She drank in his scent, felt his well-formed arms and back as she clasped him to her. Then, she pushed him away hurriedly.

"I forgot to create a charm for you, to keep you safe on your journey," she said in a near panic. "I intended to do that last night, but in the calamity it entirely slipped my mind. Clearly, there's no time to do an elaborate spell to heed off evil, but I will think of something."

She went to her herb cupboard and selected two containers. Pulling the amulet from her neck, she sat it in a bowl, covered it with the herbs, and glanced sideways at him. "This part you will not be so pleased about," she said.

"Why? What do you need?"

"Your blood."

"In what quantity?" he asked nervously.

"A drop or two should suffice."

He offered his hand. Pulling out her dagger, she sliced deeply into his third finger. He didn't flinch, and his face remained skeptical as she squeezed several drops onto the amulet. She placed the knifepoint on her thumb, but he stopped her.

"And, why is your blood needed as well?"

"Because, 'tis my amulet. It was charmed with my blood when I was an infant." She held up her thumb and showed him the scar at the base of her thumb.

"Why was that such a long, deep cut? To have left a scar that lasted a lifetime, it would have been very deep and large on an infant."

"Aye, Morag says it is because my mother would have needed a charm to last me for a lengthy time. Perhaps, she knew she was not to live long and thought it would be necessary to protect me from harm for all my life. I tried to speak of it to my father once, but he will not discuss druid beliefs or charms. I suppose, he feels it is a slight to Christianity." She cut herself with the knife and squeezed.

"And, why did you poke my finger and your thumb?"

"You'll need to use your thumb on the reins for a time, and 'twas only a practical gesture, not a ritual necessity."

When she had mixed their blood with the other ingredients, she stood back and recited words in a language foreign to him. The amulet burst into flames, and he jumped back, holding his pounding heart.

"Does it frighten you, Killian? Does my use of witchcraft disturb you?"

"Ah, well, it does leave me feeling a little uneasy, I'll admit it to you."

She removed the amulet from the bowl. The metal was blackened, but the image was still visible. She kissed it, then, placed it around his neck. "To guarantee a safe journey and to protect you from harm, Killian. But, remember you must not remove it."

"And, what will keep you safe, while I am gone? What will protect you?"

"I have my powers, though I prefer not to use them in view of others. And, besides, I will be kept entirely preoccupied with the healing and the food preparations. Cook and the steward have employed near a hundred extra peasants and villagers to assist with the food and the readying of the castle for the feast. I will have little time to find myself in any trouble."

"Aye, but you seem to find it whether you're looking for it or not, Alainn. Be cautious. Stay away from strangers. And, keep your distance from the McGilvarys and the priest. And, the witch," he added before kissing her one more time.

"Aye, I'll be cautious."

"I'll miss you greatly, Lainna. The days will seem endless without your lovely face to look upon, your lively conversations to hear. I look forward to being with you upon my return." He squeezed her tightly once more. "I'm off then."

"I shall always love you, Killian," she managed to choke out as tears brimmed in her eyes.

"And, I you, Lainna."

"God Speed!" she whispered, as he closed the door behind him.

⌘

MUCH TIME HAD passed when Alainn headed out the kitchen gate toward the herb garden. She was startled to discover the horses still standing by the stable, and the guardsmen, waiting with both Rory and Riley. Killian was nowhere to be found. Rory looked at her across the courtyard and waved. Riley turned and tipped his hat.

"Hello, Rory!" she called.

"Good morning, Alainn!" Rory exclaimed. She hurried toward them. "Good morning, Riley."

"Alainn." He nodded.

"Why have you not set off yet?"

The brothers looked at each other, but neither answered. "What is it?"

"Killian is in discussion with Father," Riley answered. "They've been in there awhile, and, by the sounds of it, 'tis not an amicable conversation."

"Aye, their voices could be heard echoing off the walls of the great hall," Rory added.

"Do you know what the disagreement is in regard to?"

She asked hesitantly.

"No, we were sent from the room. Everyone was, even the guards at the door, the steward, and the priest."

"But, you've an inkling as to what it pertains, Rory?"

"Aye, I've a notion." He lifted an eyebrow and her cheeks flushed pink. At that moment, Killian stormed out of the castle gate with his uncle not far behind. Alainn scurried to the stable, passing her father as she entered a stall beside one of the chieftain's mares. He nodded to her but did not smile. Alainn ducked down in the stall, where she could remain hidden but still hear the conversation between the men outside.

The chieftain's voice rang out, loud and authoritative. "You'll come to your senses in time, Killian! When you truly take the time to think this through, you'll realize what must be done!"

Killian did not respond. Alainn stood, risking a peek at him. His jaw was tensed, his deep green eyes filled with anger. He turned his back to his uncle and went to his horse. The older man embraced his two sons warmly before they got onto their horses. He drew nearer to Killian and opened his arms, but the young man ignored the gesture, walking around the other side of his horse to speak to Pierce, the captain's son, who had come to send them off. The chieftain's face paled and he grimaced registering the insult.

Alainn tried to hear Killian's thoughts as he spoke to Pierce, but all the emotions being emitted from the group of men cluttered her ability, and she'd never been adept at reading his mind. His stern expression indicated it was a matter of importance. He looked up briefly and she could see his deep consternation. She longed to go to him and comfort him, to smooth the concern from his face and see his wonderful green eyes fill with warmth and happiness, again.

Killian mounted his horse without a glance to his uncle. Rory and Riley bid their father good-bye and the guards all called out their respectful addresses to their chieftain. They set their heels to the horses' sides and were off, through the castle gates and over the drawbridge. She listened to the pounding of the hooves as they faded in the distance. The chieftain remained where he stood, staring in the direction of the departed riders. He wore an expression of deep vexation and Alainn didn't need to possess clairvoyant powers to know his angry thoughts were directed at her.

Chapter Twenty

ALAINN RACED TOWARD the thicket, Pierce close behind her. She was not entirely pleased. He had been accompanying her everywhere she went. Unless she was asleep in her bedchamber with Morag, he was by her side. Her personal guard, Killian had ordered him not to let her out of his sight and the young man took his task most seriously.

The day was miserable. A slow, steady drizzle had set in and the sky was a mass of dark grey clouds. The dampness made Alainn shiver and her already queasy stomach grew steadily worse. The light-headed feeling she'd been suffering had also returned and she could no longer deny the fact that she carried Killian's child.

She had tried to convince herself she'd been late before, but she recalled that was years ago, when she'd first begun her monthlies. Since then, she could detect almost to the hour when they would commence. And, she was now two weeks past due. Killian had been away for four days now. She missed him sorely, both his company and his touch. She would wake up in the night with a need within her, one she had never felt till she and Killian had become lovers. Now, she yearned for the physical intimacy they shared.

She had been plagued by a most disturbing dream, the past two nights, and it had caused her to sleep fitfully. In her dream, Killian stared adoringly, passionately, at a tall, dark-haired woman. She had lovely curls and large brown eyes that shone warmly when she looked back at Killian. At first, Alainn believed it was only her jealousy at Killian's affinity for the French women they'd spoken of. He'd seemed most fond of their dark hair and eyes. But, now, she was not so certain. Although her dreams were not as accurate as her visions, they often held a truth of what would take place sometime in the future. She shivered again and pulled the hood of her cloak tightly over her head.

Though she usually welcomed a time in the wooded area beyond the castle, today she was displeased with having to make the journey into the woods. Since Morag had fallen gravely ill two days previously, she had spent most of her time sitting by her side. Cook was very understanding, knowing her place was with Morag. However, this morning when Mrs. O'Leary had come to the kitchen in search of Morag or Alainn, Cookson had come to retrieve her.

The woman's four small children had been scourged with a bright red, noticeably itchy rash and she needed a balm to relieve their discomfort. The same occurrence had happened the two previous years when the small red berries were found growing wild and the children had eaten them. Most times, Alainn would have the balm ready in anticipation of the need. But, her mind had been so filled with thoughts of Killian, the predicament she found herself in, and Morag's failing health that she had allowed many of her herbal remedies to dwindle. She thought her powers of perception usually aided her in times when her mind was filled with other thoughts, but they, too, seemed to be lacking.

A trip to the herb garden would have taken no time, but, unfortunately, the type of ground ivy needed to produce the balm grew wild in the thicket. Alainn had tried to cultivate it and produce it in the herb garden, but it was more suited to the shady area of the forest where it flourished.

Pierce had remained quiet for the entire walk into the trees. She felt slightly guilty at his silence, for earlier, when he had insisted on accompanying her but complained about the need for the lengthy walk on such a rain-filled day, she had snapped at him. She had apologized, but he had said very little since then. To be truthful, she knew how irritable she'd been the last few days. Lack of sleep accounted for most of it, but, she had to admit, the dreams of Killian with another woman were leaving her less than cheerful. She wondered why this woman came to her dreams in such clarity, when she knew she'd never seen her before. And, now, that there was a child to be considered, and, even though it was doomed by the witch's curse, she found herself filled with uncertainty.

As Alainn bent to the bushes to retrieve the ivy she'd come for, she found herself overcome with a vision. She saw

Pierce lying on the ground with her dagger in his chest. Her stomach heaved and her head became fuzzy. She leaned against a nearby tree for fear she would faint. Pierce put his arm around her, steadying her.

She would never strike Pierce with her analace. He would never attempt anything dishonorable, surely not when Killian had ordered him to watch over her. But, she had little time to wonder what the vision meant before voices approached. They turned to see the McGilvary brothers coming their way. Pierce stiffened. He was a fair swordsman, having improved greatly with instruction from Killian and the captain, and the McGilvarys were not noted for their skills in that area, but they were unscrupulous. Alainn felt her chilled feeling deepen. The brothers advanced nearer and Alainn placed her hand in her apron pocket to grasp the dagger within.

"What are the two of you doing out and about on such an unpleasant day?" Pierce demanded.

"Hunting," Henry simply said.

"What game would be out this morning?"

"We've tracked nothing until now," the younger brother sneered wickedly.

"Just go back to the village," Pierce directed, "for we've not seen any game about this day. Sure, they're all jumpy and skittish since the chieftain has had his huntsmen busy with finding adequate meat for the feasts."

" 'Tis not the four legged game we're after, this day,"

Richard McGilvary declared. "And, besides, what are the two of you doing here so thick in the woods? I thought it was only the chieftain's sons and nephew that the wench provided services for."

"You close your vile mouth, Richard McGilvary. There's no need to make trouble. You've been warned to keep your distance from women."

"Aye, but who is going to stop us? Do you think you can best the two of us?"

Pierce puffed out his chest and stood taller. "Aye! I could take the both of you, with one arm tied behind my back."

"Pierce," Alainn hissed, "don't encourage them, 'tis what they want."

"Oh, Alainn McCreary, I think you've a fairly good idea of what we want," Richard McGilvary drawled.

The two men started toward them and Pierce drew his sword. The older brother unsheathed his sword and held it ready. The younger kept walking toward Alainn. She stepped back, gripping the dagger in her pocket. The clang of steel on steel alerted her that Pierce was now actively in swordplay with the older lad. The other was within a few feet of her. He leered at her with such a lecherous expression she felt her stomach knot. He had a knife in his hand. Pierce barely blocked a heavy swing to his head as he looked her way with concern. The sword swooshed through the air close to his head.

"Just deal with him, Pierce," cried Alainn. "Keep your

eyes only on him!"

"Aye, you keep him occupied for a time," sneered Richard, "and the farrier's daughter and I will spend time getting to know one another better." His hand was already on the fastenings of his trews and the repulsion she felt made her stomach reel. Bile rose in her throat and she turned, certain she would soon lose what little breakfast she had ingested. The young man lunged at her as dizziness overtook her. The thought went through her mind that Killian would not be here to save her this day, when the world went black.

⌘

WHEN SHE AWOKE, Henry McGilvary was holding his arm. Blood was seeping from a cut in his shirt. Pierce had obviously stuck him with his sword. She looked around for Pierce, praying he hadn't been killed. He was behind her, looking as pale as a spirit. The other younger brother lay on the ground, her dagger in his thigh. Pierce helped her to her feet.

Both offenders were in obvious pain, but Richard wore an expression of hatred that he directed at Alainn.

"What type of sorcery did you use on me?" he screamed.

Alainn looked helplessly at Pierce, but he would not answer. Instead, he picked up her basket, took her arm, and led her toward the opening in the trees.

"What just happened, Pierce?" she demanded, once they were a suitable distance from the others.

"I'm not certain, Alainn. Richard was nearly on top of you, when I cut Henry with my sword. I tried to get to you, when he was thrown from you by a force unseen, and, when he tried to get up, the dagger flew out of your hand as though you had aimed it, but you were clearly unconscious. It barely missed me. I cannot say what magic helped us this day, Alainn, but it is to be thanked for you not being harmed. Sorry, I am that I could not keep them away from you. I should not have taunted them when I know how evil and dangerous they can be. Forgive me, Alainn. Killian will have my head on a platter for not seeing you safe."

"He needn't know, then, Pierce."

"How can we keep it from him? He will surely suspect when he learns of their wounds."

"I doubt they'll be eager to tell anyone of this incident. They will hardly come to me for healing assistance. Perhaps, we'll be fortunate and they'll die from their wounds," she seethed.

She stopped and cursed under her breath. They'd left without retrieving her weapon. She closed her eyes, called to her powers, and summoned the dagger to her. There was a bellowing scream as the anelace ripped itself from McGilvary's flesh, and, with a whoosh, the knife sliced through the trees like an arrow, dropping lightly into her hand. Pierce glanced at her with horror and crossed himself, before turning away.

Chapter Twenty-One

ALAINN WAS WAKENED by the same dream she'd had the previous nights, of a dark-haired woman with warm, brown eyes. She could not fall back asleep no matter how weary and fatigued she felt, for it had left her worrisome.

She'd sat by Morag's side for half the night, fearful the woman would die without waking. The old healer seemed to be barely conscious any longer. Alainn thought it would be a kindness if she slipped away in her sleep, for, when awake, her breathing was raspier and she appeared to be in great discomfort. Morag, in one coherent moment, had asked that she be allowed to pass on without further benefit of healing.

She still had not spoken to Alainn of any secrets. Now, although she seemed to want to talk, she was unable to convey the message she had intended. When Morag had finally drifted to sleep, Alainn had crept to her own bed to seek rest, at least for a short while. It was nearly dawn and Killian would be arriving at the castle soon. Perhaps, on the morrow, or the day following. She needed him desperately to hold her and comfort her. Although she'd decided she wouldn't tell him of her condition, she felt her resolve waning when she remembered Mara's regret that her child's father had not been allowed to be with his child.

How could she keep the knowledge from Killian when she loved him so completely? Yet, telling him would surely prove nothing. He would lose his title and all hope of becoming chieftain. And, the child would not live past a day or two. That thought tore at Alainn's heart, for she was becoming attached to the unborn child that grew within her. How could she bear to carry this child to term and then have it ripped from her life because of Mara's curse? No, she would not tell Killian and have his heart broken, as well.

The unsettling incident with the McGilvarys continued to deeply disturb her. She had very nearly been raped, and, as loathsome as the thought was, she also despaired that she had used her witchcraft while unconscious. She could have stabbed Pierce with the weapon, as she had seen in her vision. How could she control a weapon if she could not recall using her powers? That was a danger she could ill afford to repeat. And, she'd been foolish to use her magic in Pierce's presence. Her mind felt dizzy with uneasy thoughts.

Morag moaned in her sleep. Alainn dragged herself from the bed, wrapped a thick shawl around her shoulders, and went to sit on the chair beside the old woman's bed. She opened her eyes, but Alainn was uncertain if she was truly aware of her presence.

Gently taking her hand, she squeezed it and whispered, "You may go, Morag. Do not hold on for me. I am a woman now and will find my way, on my own. You have taught me well. Don't remain here in this world of pain. I will send you off with a thank you for all you have done. You have been the only mother I have ever known, and I would not wish for another had I the chance."

The older woman squeezed her hand and tried to talk.

"You must go to the farrier," she rasped in a voice that was barely audible. "You must ask him to explain the truth. Tell him I have instructed you to do so."

"He barely speaks to me, Morag."

"Tell him it is time. The boy has died. It is time."

"I don't understand, Morag. What does Mara's son have to do with the secret?"

"You will see, my caileag leanabh. Sorry, I am, that I won't be here to see you through the uncertain days ahead."

Tears spilled down Alainn's cheeks. "I carry a child, Morag. And, I know not what's to be done about it."

The woman patted her hand sympathetically. "Will you take the herbs to root the child from you?"

"No, Morag. I cannot, for I love the father dearly. I cannot destroy what our love has created."

"Those are the words spoken to me by your, by Mara, not so very long ago, and she has suffered because of it. You carry an O'Brien within you, so you will suffer ten-fold when the child is taken from you. Go to Mara. When you know the truth, go to her and find a way to have the curse lifted. Perhaps she'll manage it ...." The woman's voice faded. Pain tightened her face. She clutched her chest and squeezed the girl's hand, once more. The raspy breaths stilled, and quiet filled the room.

She laid her head on the old woman's chest and wept till she could weep no more.

⌘

ALAINN SAT IN the kitchen with Cook and Molly. Her face was swollen and stained with tears. Her hair, askew. The smell of food was making her nauseous, but she couldn't bear the thought of going back to the empty bedchamber. Molly was weeping in earnest and held Alainn's hand tightly. "Don't cry, Molly," she said wearily. "You didn't even like Morag."

Alainn touched the younger girl's arm.

" 'Twas not that I didn't like her, she frightened me, is all. And, I weep for you, Alainn. Now you have no one, but our family." Molly threw her arms around Alainn in a tight hug. "You must come live with us, now, Alainn. Father, may she come live with us?"

"Aye, if it is as you would like it. You may stay with us, Alainn."

She looked up at the kind man but knew it was not a likelihood. Cook and his large family had little room in their small home. He often needed to take home the scraps from the kitchen just to feed his family. It was only a few months previously that the steward had talked to Cook about his pilfering from the chieftain. He had suggested Cook and his family looked to be most robust, that they must surely be taking more than their share of the provisions allowed for the kitchen staff. Alainn had intervened and told the steward he could come spend his days in the kitchen to see what type of food was taken by the servants and what quality. The man had left, but she knew he had been dissatisfied with her explanation. Alainn could not impose another worry upon Cook.

She had yet to go to the farrier. Though she was undeniably curious about the secret Morag had kept for such a long time, she was hesitant to learn it. She had made up her mind to go after Morag was laid to rest. The chieftain intended to have Morag buried in the cemetery beyond the west solar, and Alainn was pleased by the decision. While not the chieftain's private graveyard, the cemetery was reserved for servants who had been regarded respectfully. Servants of lesser importance were interred in Potter's field, a much darker, drearier place. Morag would be honored to lie in the western field, close to the herb garden.

This thought had barely crossed her mind when Morag's spirit was beside her. She looked old, as she had been just before death, but no longer bent or frail. Her eyes were clear, once more, and her hands, no longer twisted. Alainn was filled with joy and smiled brightly at the woman. Cook glanced at her with a peculiar expression, but said nothing. Alainn knew she must speak with Morag. She begged time alone and headed for the room where the herbs were kept, for Pierce would find her if she left the castle. She closed the door and locked it.

"Oh, Morag, I am truly gladdened you have come to me. I thought I would never see you or speak with you, again." She attempted to embrace the old woman but her arms passed through air.

"You must go to the farrier! You need to do this, now."

"I am not eager to do so, Morag. Tell me this secret. I desire to hear it from you."

"Aye, but the farrier knows the tale in its entirety. It is best heard through him."

"No, Morag—" she protested, but the hazy apparition disappeared and she stood, once more alone. Alainn sighed. She had little choice but to go to her father and ask what truths he had hidden within his mind.

Chapter Twenty-Two

I N APPEARANCE, THE old man was not much younger than
Morag. He stood, grooming the chieftain's stallion, when
she went to him. Though clearly not delighted to see her, he
did not seem surprised. Pierce waited outside the stable
though he was not happy about that arrangement. Her father
busied himself with the horse, barely looking at her. She
found herself longing for a father who did not feel so little
toward her.

"You know of Morag's passing," she began.

"Aye, I've heard."

He continued brushing the horse, saying nothing further
to his daughter.

"Morag has instructed me to ask you what secret you
keep," she said impatiently. He glanced at her briefly but
soon returned to his currying. "I am not overjoyed to spend
this time with you either!" she snapped. "So, tell me what
must be said, and I will trouble you no longer!"

The old man sighed deeply and Alainn thought he would
refuse to answer, but he set down his brush and looked,
really looked at her, as if for the first time.

"You do not resemble your mother," he said. "The eyes, perhaps, are somewhat similar, but that is the extent of it."

"Though I am well pleased to have you actually speak of my mother to me, I hardly think a physical resemblance to your wife is a deep, dark secret."

"You have a bitter tongue, girl."

"Please, tell me what it is I am to learn from you."

He hesitated, then, sighed. "We thought we could take you for our own," he said with a shrug. "We promised her we would. You were pink and healthy, and a pretty wee thing, even then."

Alainn swallowed hard as she heard these words, but waited for the man to continue.

"She came to us the night our son was born. Only minutes before he was born. The midwife was busy helping the cook's wife, for it was when she delivered her twin boys. My wife was elderly, she had a difficult birth. We were alone and frightened, and when the witch came to the door and offered to help, we allowed it, even knowing she was banished from the castle and the village. Our baby boy was so still, we thought he would not live. He was blue, and his face and body were twisted and malformed. He did not breathe. He did not cry. She placed her hands on him and he breathed, and then he cried. All the while, you lay in the basket beside the witch.

"She convinced us our boy would be taunted and misunderstood if he remained with us in the village. She told us she would keep him safe and tend to his abnormalities, for she was a healer, as well. In exchange, we would keep her girl child. A healthy, normal, beautiful baby girl. You were bright, even then. Two days-old, you were, when you came to live with us. The witch said, if you remained with her, you would be made to pay for her mistakes, and you would never know a normal life. Our son would never be capable of leading a normal life. And, so, we agreed.

"She wrapped him up and allowed my wife to hold him for but a moment. She placed her amulet around your neck and cried as many tears as my wife. The exchange was made and we were made to promise that we would raise you as our own. We were to call you Alainn, she said."

Alainn was shaking. She touched her cheeks. They were wet.

"Sorry, I am, that I couldn't be a father to you. After my wife died, I had no knowledge of how to raise a child, especially a girl-child. And, when you started working your magic, I could have no more part of you. I believed you would turn out like she did." Sobs rose in her throat, wanting to be released, so she only nodded to the man she had believed to be her father.

"You know your son has passed," she finally managed to utter.

"Aye."

"I was with him when he left this earth, and many times through the years."

"I did not know that," he said in a weak and emotionless voice.

"Aye, and he was happy and content with the mind of a child all his life. The witch treated him kindly. She was correct in assuming he would have been subjected to much cruelty if he'd been in close contact with others."

"Aye, I know it, but 'tis still a guilt I cannot bear, to know we gave away our only child, to be raised by someone we believed evil."

"He is at peace, now." She paused a moment before asking, "Did she tell you who my father is?"

"No, she would not say. I suppose that is something you must discuss with her."

"Aye, I've much to discuss with her. I must borrow a horse."

"The chieftain's sons and nephew have taken the horses you usually ride, but there is the mare you helped heal, if you want to take her."

"Aye, and I thank you."

"The chieftain will be most vexed if he learns I have allowed it."

"I doubt it would be you that would suffer because of it at any rate." Alainn mounted the horse.

"You don't want benefit of saddle or bridle?" the farrier asked.

"I've no time for them. If the captain's son asks where I have gone, tell him you don't know, would you, please?"

"Aye, I suppose I owe you that much." He watched as Alainn galloped off through the back gate of the stable.

⌘

IT WAS A long ride through the stone close and around the fairy glade, but Alainn would not attempt to make the trip through the glade without her amulet. The jet-black mare beneath her seemed willing to gallop wildly though the open meadow.

She had healed the mare when she was just a foal. It had been born frail, not expected to live. The chieftain had ordered it destroyed and Alainn had been in the stable when the guard had come to do the deed, but she had stood in front of it, refusing to move. She told the guard he would have to kill her first. When the guard left to speak to the farrier, she had placed her hands on it. Within minutes, it was as healthy as any foal in the stables. The chieftain had been in great disbelief of this event, and Rory had tried to persuade his father the horse should belong to Alainn because she had healed it. He would not hear of it. Two years later, when it had fallen and broken its leg while the chieftain was riding it, she had healed it again, so, she thought of it as hers for she'd saved its life twice. She named it Magic. Only Killian and the twins knew of her pet name for the horse. Magic was fond of Alainn, as well. They had ridden together on a few occasions.

Now, the horse galloped on, clearly pleased with the rid-er and the speed. Alainn untied her hair and felt it being tossed and blown by the wind. How quickly her world had changed. When she drew nearer to the caves where the witch lived, she became apprehensive, tormented by her confused emotions.

The witch was waiting for her. By the look on her face, she apparently knew what she had come for.

Chapter Twenty-Three

"So, Morag has passed and you know the truth," she said simply. "I am your mother."

Alainn dismounted her horse and glowered. "Why did you not tell me the truth before?" she spat out.

"The time was not right. You needed to live in the castle, grow into the fine young woman you are. Though you clearly don't accept me now, it would have been more confusing to you if you'd learned the truth as a child."

"How could you just give me away?" she asked, her voice breaking.

The older woman's eyes brimmed with tears, but she lifted her chin as she spoke. "It was the most difficult thing I have ever done, and I have been forced to do many difficult things. I had planned it for some time, for months before you were born. I knew the farrier's wife carried a child that would not be normal, a child that may not live. I used my powers to see it, for, when I worked as a healer, I assisted many people as you now do."

"Did you see that the child would not be healthy or did you make it so?"

"You believe me that evil?"

"How many O'Brien babies have you caused to die? At least a dozen, I would suspect. You think you are not evil?"

"I have told you, I much regret that. Hugh O'Brien's wife, Lady Siobhan was always very kind to me. I would not have chosen to make her suffer in any way, but, after the words were spoken, I could not rectify them, nor have I been able to all these years."

"Who is my father?"

"No one you know. He is not from here, but he is of noble birth."

Alainn felt her stomach lurch. She lowered herself to the rocks, her head spinning.

Mara dared to sit upon the rock beside Alainn as she spoke. "Are you well, Alainn? What has come over you?"

"Tell me I am not in love with my brother. Tell me that I don't carry my brother's child!"

"You are with child?" Mara gasped. "Answer me!"

"You are not an O'Brien." Alainn sagged with relief. "What would make you think you are?"

"You said my father is of noble blood, and you admitted knowing Kieran O'Brien. You said he was a good man."

"Aye, and he was. He was a friend to your father."

"Then, you must tell me who he is."

"There is no need in you knowing who he is. There is no way of proving it, and he has been gone from my life since soon after we learned you were growing within me. Not by his choice or by mine, but by the O'Brien's doing."

"So, I am never to know my paternity?"

"That is the least of your concerns, I would suggest. How did you end up being with child?"

"The usual way, I suspect."

"You have a bitter tongue, Alainn."

"Aye, and you're not the first to tell me that this day."

"You know of the herbs that prevent pregnancy. You are well aware what helps in preventing an unwanted child."

"I did not plan to be intimate with Killian. It happened, and I was not regretful of it."

"So, you have hope the child will live, even knowing about the curse?"

"Aye, I suppose I am fool-hearted, but I must have hope. Why are you flaying me about carrying a child? You were scarcely older than I am now."

"Because, it is not an easy undertaking, raising a child by yourself!"

"If you cannot alter the curse, I suppose that won't be a consideration for me. Will it?"

They sat in silence for some time.

"You have no other questions?" Mara asked.

"Aye, I have a thousand, I would estimate, but am not certain where to begin. Tell me of your parents, then. Morag was never willing to discuss your mother, though I know she raised her, as well."

"Aye, Morag raised her from a tiny infant. No one knows

for certain where she came from. She was left at the castle gates in a basket. They were able to make it through the palisade and across the drawbridge without the guards being aware of it."

"Perhaps, they were magical beings."

"Aye, 'tis what Morag supposed. And, my mother bore the mark of the fairies."

"She was a tweenling?"

"Aye, it is a likelihood. She was probably the product of a fairy and human union, born between the realms."

"Was she tiny of stature?"

"No smaller than you and me, I am told, though, I never knew her. She died in childbed when birthing me."

"The father must have been of giant girth, then, or the mother a fairy princess, for, they are often largest of the fairies."

"Aye, I have done much pondering on the subject throughout my life. 'Tis surely where our magical powers come from."

"So, we are not truly witches but of fairy origin."

"Perhaps, though most witches' magic comes from the realm of the fairies. 'Tis only mislabeled."

"Why did Morag never wish to speak of your mother, my grandmother? I don't even know her name."

"It was Ainna, named for the defender of women. And, Morag loved her dearly, as if she were her own child. She was a lovely girl, I am told, of a kind and good demeanor. Morag often tried to compare her to me. She said I was surely far too stubborn and pig-headed to resemble my mother. She felt I must have inherited my father's traits."

"And, who was your father?"

"You'll not favor that any more than the fact I am your mother. Your grandfather was a McKenna! You are the granddaughter of a McKenna, the O'Briens' mortal enemy. Their bitter feud has been going on for centuries."

Alainn closed her eyes and shook her head. "Was she raped? Was the child a result of a forceful union?"

"No, Morag always said they were desperately in love. There had been a battle. The McKennas had come in attempt to reclaim the castle that was once theirs. My father was wounded and managed to make it into the fairy glade."

"He entered the glade? Was he of magical ancestry, as well?"

"Perhaps, though it was between Beltane and Samhain, so the portals may have been open. However he came to be there, my mother found him. She healed him and nursed him back to good health. They fell in love and I was conceived."

"You were conceived during Samhain?"

"Aye, so my powers are great. But, not as great as yours. You were born during Samhain."

"And, what became of him, my grandfather?"

"It is not known for certain. One day, he was simply gone. My mother feared the O'Briens had found him and murdered him. Morag thought, perhaps, he went through one of the portals in the glade. My mother never believed he would have just left her, for, apparently their love was great. Morag always believed she died as much of a broken heart as from childbirth. She said she only waited until I was born to allow me to live, but that she could not bear to live without her love."

"So, it would appear our line is fated to be alone and heartbroken." Mara shrugged. "You may yet have a chance at happiness."

"I don't see how. Killian is surely to wed a woman of noble birth. I am your daughter, and you are a McKenna, too. And, I will not have him bear the pain of losing his child."

"But, you are of noble paternity. Perhaps, if we can prove that, if you are accepted into nobility and marry the man you seem to care for so deeply, then the curse would be remedied."

"You said there is no way to prove my paternity, and, even if there were, I would be considered illegitimate, and I am the daughter of the woman who cursed their line. They cannot learn one without the other."

"Aye, there are many quandaries and many obstacles to overcome." Mara thought hard for a moment, then exclaimed, "There is the amulet!"

"My amulet?"

"Aye, it belonged to your father. He gave it to me. There is another portion that belongs with it. They were melded together, but when I was taken to the dungeon, after I cursed the O'Brien, I smashed it against the rock wall until it broke and then hid it behind a stone in the dungeon wall. I knew the chieftain and his priest would take it from me. It has your father's crest upon it. It will prove that you are his."

"I don't see how, it would only prove you had the man's amulet. You could have stolen it from him. It does nothing to prove I am his or even yours. And, there is still the fact I was born out of wedlock."

"That is not entirely true," said Mara. Alainn looked up sharply. "We were wed, secretly wed, only the priest and Killian's father know of it. After Killian's father and his family returned to their home, when the O'Brien discovered the truth, the priest denied marrying us. Your father was furious and threatened the chieftain. He was taken away. I still know not what became of him, whether he lives or not. I think, if he lived, he would have come back for me. I believe that within my heart."

"So, the priest knows the truth? No wonder I have always found his aura so dark. He must be made to tell this chieftain the truth, for surely he would not be as horrid as his father was."

"Do not be so certain, Alainn. I have never trusted him. While he has always seemed more honorable than his father, he will surely do what is best for the O'Briens. And, if anyone learns I was wed to a noble, an acquaintance of the O'Briens, he would surely do most anything to conceal that information. There are many matters to be considered, but the other piece of the amulet must be found before anything else can be done. Since I am not allowed near the castle, and the guards are ordered to aim their arrows straight for my heart should I attempt it, it is surely up to you to locate it."

"You would have me sent to the dungeon?"

"Aye, not by choice. But, if it is the only way to save your child, it would be worth the punishment."

"But, a trip to the dungeon usually involves lashes or a beating!" she exclaimed, horrified at the thought. "Sure that would not be beneficial to the child."

"I am well aware what it involves. I've lived through that and more, and so did you, for I carried you at the time. If and when you are ready to consider it, I will instruct you further as to where the metal crest is located."

Alainn looked up at the sky. The sun was low in the west. She had spent far too much time with Mara. Though the crime of horse-thievery might only have her thrown in the dungeon, it was also possible she would be hanged for the offense. She skillfully mounted while her mother looked on.

"I have never regretted your birth, Alainn. Many times, I have been disheartened at being parted from you, but never have I wished you had not been born. When you began visiting me of your own accord, I was overjoyed to see you, to watch you grow. So confident and beautiful, and intellect so rare. I took pride in what a fine girl you were and, now, I marvel at the wonderful woman you have become. You may never forgive me for sending you away, but you would have been ostracized as I am. I do not regret leaving you that night, so many years ago. Though, when the woman who had promised to be your mother could not manage it, I was forced to rectify the situation."

"How do you know she was not a mother to me?"

"I summoned her reflection many times in the well in the cave. She would barely pick you up. She would not feed you. They employed a wet nurse to see you nourished."

"There is another who knows of our secret."

"No, she no longer lives."

"You caused her death?" Alainn gasped.

"Aye, and the farrier's wife, as well. She was afflicted with a malady of the mind, a melancholia. Perhaps due to guilt for trading her child for mine, or the sadness that oft accompanies the birth of a babe. I am not certain. She wept constantly and eventually confided the secret to the wet nurse. A tea laced in poison shared by the two ensured no one else learned the truth!"

"My God, you are evil! How can I ever think of you as a mother when I know what evil you have done?"

"They conspired to take your life, Alainn. After the wet nurse learned the secret she suggested they drown you in the nearby pond to ensure you did not grow to be as evil as me. The farrier's wife feared me and knew I cared for her son, so did not agree to it straightaway, but it was surely only a matter of time in her maudlin state before she listened to the other woman, or before the woman spread the word to others. I needed to protect you. I was forced to take drastic action!"

Alainn stared at the other woman a flurry of muddled emotions swirling in her mind and tearing at her heart! "Though you may have done the deeds in order to protect me, I cannot accept the fact you ended the lives of two women."

"You are not yet a mother, my dear, Alainn. You know not what you'll do in the name of protecting your child."

"I pray I will be given the chance to know what it is to be a mother to care for my child, to see the child born healthy and to live a long life. I understand your sacrifice in giving me away so that I would have a better life, but I find it difficult to accept the fact you committed murder."

"People do much to protect their kin."

"I cannot be here with you any longer. Perhaps, in time, I will forgive you for abandoning me," she said, turning her horse away, "but not this day."

Mara watched the girl gallop off. "I am willing to begin with that," she whispered.

Chapter Twenty-Four

AFTER ANOTHER SLEEPLESS night, Alainn met the morning, exhausted, miserable, and on the verge of tears. She'd spent the first half of the night dwelling on all she had learned, unable to fall asleep. When sleep finally came to her, she dreamed of Killian and his dark-haired woman, of fairies and evil witches. She awoke in a cold sweat with her nightdress soaked through and wept into her pillow. How she longed for Morag to talk to, for Killian to hold her. When she stood to dress, her empty stomach heaved and she spewed bile into the basin. Weak and jittery, and extremely dizzy, the thought of entering the kitchen to eat left her hanging over the basin, again.

Tomorrow, Morag would be laid to rest. It seemed an eternity had passed since Killian had left and Morag had died. She missed them both, unbearably.

"You must take nourishment, caileag leanabh," Morag said by her ear. The spectral woman was standing next to her. "The child cannot grow if you refuse to eat. Go to the herb room. You know very well what aids in relieving the morning sickness. You're not thinking straight. Laurel, mint,

marigold, ginger, or nutmeg. Go dose yourself, immediately."

"Morag, I need to talk to you. We have much to discuss."

"Now is not the time, caileag. You have a most difficult
day ahead of you. Make haste."

"Don't go—" But, the old woman had disappeared.
Alainn despaired at the ominous warning, but she listened to
Morag. She ground the herbs and made a hot tea. She sipped
it slowly, leaning against the cool stone wall, waiting for her
stomach to quit protesting and her head to stop spinning.

Cook stuck his head in the door and offered a sympa-
thetic look. She felt the tears nearly brimming, once more.
He brought her some soda bread and she nodded to him but
did not move. How empathetic she would be the next time a
woman suffering from the morning malady came to her for a
cure. Some women seemed to never suffer the ill stomach,
but Morag had always insisted women who suffered with the
nausea almost never miscarried.

When she'd managed to keep half a piece of bread down
without gagging, she considered herself most fortunate. The
thought of entering the kitchen was still an unpleasant
consideration, so she dared to take a moment longer to
remain immobile. She was startled by a knock on the outside
door. Thinking Killian may have returned, she bounded to
the door and swung it open. Two guards stood, peering
down at her with grim faces.

"You are to come with us," the senior guard stated. "The chieftain wishes you to take audience with him this morning."

Alainn's heart skipped and began pounding loudly. She tried to use her powers to detect the chieftain's thoughts but could not. The men waited for her to obey their command.

"Cook! I must go out for a time!" she called.

He came to the door and saw the two guards. "What is it you need?" he asked almost fearfully.

"Just the girl. She is to come with us."

"Has there been some trouble?"

"We know none of the details, only that she is to come with us."

"By whose orders?"

"Earl O'Brien has ordered it and he is waiting, so, you'd best comply without further delay, girl." The man roughly grabbed her arm and Cook started toward him.

"Don't interfere, Cook!" Alainn cried putting up her hand. She added more calmly, "It is the chieftain's orders, so we must comply."

"I will be waiting to see you when you return," he said, trying to smile, though his face showed his unease at the turn of events.

⌘

THE GUARDS ESCORTED Alainn into the great hall and she felt slight relief that she had not been escorted to the chieftain's bedchamber in the north solar. She stepped through the doorway but could scarcely make her feet move further. The room was immense and most intimidating. The guards released her arms and the chieftain's loud voice boomed across the wide expanse. "Leave her here with me and return to your posts outside the door!"

"Yes, Milord!" They bowed low and walked backward, in deep respect of the earl. The large wooden door creaked, then, clunked shut, the sound echoing off the massive walls.

The room was of gargantuan proportions, the ceiling, three stories high. The length of the room was equal to the sporting field where bouts and training were held. Alainn had only been there once before, and it had seemed much less intimidating, then. A statue of a man on horseback stood at the far end of the room and many hunting trophies adorned the walls. Wolves, red deer, wild boar, bear heads. They hung in great numbers, their eyes staring down at her in a most disturbing manner. The horns of deer hung at one end of the hall. The enormous antlers of the giant Irish elk, a creature long since gone from this world, hung at the other. Alainn remembered seeing that set of impressive antlers being pulled from a peat bog when she was a child. The chieftain had been most pleased. It was the largest they'd ever seen. It hung above the gigantic table where the chieftain now sat.

Sometimes, when she entered a room, especially of this age and this size, Alainn could hear the echo of past times and long ago events. If it was quiet enough, she could hear conversations that had taken place centuries before. There was much to be heard in this room.

Alainn attempted to still the spectral voice of a man pleading for his life, the echoing of painful screams, the sound of a lash connecting with skin. She forced herself to close her mind to these sounds. She could not allow herself to be distracted from what possible peril she faced.

The chieftain stared at her from across the vast expanse but did not speak. Alainn tried to keep her knees from trembling. She had never been alone with the chieftain. When she was a small child, she remembered being in Lady Siobhan's bedchamber when he had come in. Lady Siobhan was brushing her long hair and singing to her. When the chieftain entered the room, he was most displeased. His voice had been loud and angry, and she'd been made to leave. He'd never spoken to her before. He did so now. "Well don't just stand there, woman," he commanded. "Come closer so that I might see you."

Alainn willed her legs to move. She glanced around the room. A fire crackled in the enormous hearth that served to warm the hulking room, but there were no other persons present. It was entirely unusual. Almost always, the priest or the steward would attend the chieftain. The captain of the guard was often in the chieftain's company, as well, and though she didn't know for certain how the chieftain kept his hall instead of though she didn't know entirely how the chieftain kept his hall.

As she moved closer to the table, she felt the heat of the fire. A large jug sat on the table beside the chieftain, a goblet, in his hand. His cheeks were ruddy and his eyes bleary from the drink. The man had obviously been drinking. Since it was only mid-morning, he'd surely had an early start.

The chieftain had been a handsome man, at one time. He looked similar to his son, Riley, who was a handsome lad. The chieftain maintained a full head of black hair, and his broad chest and shoulders indicated he was still a powerful man. His skin was leathery, now, and his brow, lined with deep furrows. His eyes were deep brown, like Riley's, but Alainn could sense no warmth in them as they stared at her. The glow that surrounded him was dark. When she was a child, his aura had been orange in color. Today, it was a dark, murky rust. She shivered, despite the heat behind her back.

"The Maiden McCreary," he drawled, "in the flesh. Finally, we meet, after all the ranting of my family. I thought, perhaps, to have a goddess in my hall. Get over here, girl. You're still half a field away from me!"

She stepped closer to the table. He raked his eyes over her while she stood silently, detesting every moment. He rose and walked around to her side of the table. Her heart pounded in her throat. He pulled the cap from her head and untied her hair. It spilled down her back to her waist. He placed his face to her hair and inhaled deeply.

"Ah, you have a sweet smell about you."

" 'Tis the herbs I use to wash it, your wife uses just the same concoction."

He stepped back at the mention of his wife, but his eyes remained fixed on her. He walked back and forth behind her appraising her form.

"Do you know the consternation you have caused me through the years?" he asked.

"Me?" She jumped, startled.

"Aye, you, Alainn McCreary. The farrier's daughter. You should have been of no consequence to me, but that has not been the case. From the time your father came to me and told me he could not keep you, that he hoped I would find him a suitable family to raise you, that was when it all began. If I'd known then what I know now, I would have had you fed to the hogs while your bones were still soft!"

She lowered her eyes to the floor.

"My wife was present at the time, and he had the audacity to bring you with him when he asked me what he should do with you. My wife wanted you, not as a servant, not as a handmaiden who would one day attend to her needs, but as our child. The very thought was absurd to me, but not to her. She had just lost a fourth baby in so many years, the only daughter we would ever have born to us. She was grieving, so saddened I could not console her, and she so wanted you. Said you reminded her of her sister who had died in childhood. Begged me to allow her to raise you. How could I have allowed it? A common servant living in our home, being raised with our boys, with the O'Briens. I flatly refused, and no amount of her begging and weeping would convince me otherwise. She never forgave me for that."

He continued to pace behind her, glaring at her with something close to hatred in his eyes.

"And, so, when she wanted you to spend time with her and our sons, since you had no siblings, I relented, and it was so. I could see no harm in it. You were a very pretty, innocent child, and the lads seemed entertained by you. So, it carried on, for a time. Then my nephew suffered his tragic ordeal and he was not expected to live. But, you healed him. Whether it was truly so, or only that my wife and old Morag believed it to be so, he recovered at any rate. He was as dear to me as my own two boys and, I think, perhaps, even I felt gratitude toward you.

"Then, my lady fought me most admirably on the subject of having you schooled with our sons, with Killian and the other lads. I was against the very idea! Having a woman, a commoner take lessons with the chieftain's sons was unthinkable! But, Killian wanted it, as well. And, at the time, he wanted nothing bar going to his grave. So, that became a reality. And, then, there were the pleadings to have you attend feasts and family events. I began to tire of hearing even your name.

"When my son, then ten and three wept like a baby because I would not allow him to present you with that damnable mare, I thought to have you taken out and tossed in a peat bog where no one would have been the wiser. And believe me, that thought has crossed my mind on more than one occasion since. In truth, I have desired it many times in these past days."

"You see your son's sensitive nature as a flaw?" she asked incredulously. " 'Tis most certainly a flaw in a chieftain! How can he carry out judgments and punishments if he weeps over a lowly servant having no worldly possessions? You dare to pretend you know my sons! Do you know them?

"Or, should I say, have they known you? Is that why they hang about you so readily? Have you been in their beds?" He leered at her.

"I have not!" she cried furiously. He laughed unpleasantly. "Though you may be disinclined to believe it, your sons are my friends, and, aye, I know what type of men they are. I know their personalities, their favorable traits, and their shortcomings."

"You dare insinuate my sons have shortcomings! To my face, you would tell me this!" he screamed, his face red with rage. "In truth, I own you!"

"I am no slave!"

Chapter Twenty-Five

"YOU THINK NOT. But, I control every aspect of your life. It is in my castle you sleep, my food you eat, my herb garden you tend. I can take all of it away from you whenever I choose." He snapped his fingers by her head.

"But, there are many who need my services as a healer, especially now that Morag is no longer here."

"Aye, I was saddened to hear of her passing." His voice softened. "I give you my condolences on that regard, for she was a mother to you, I suppose."

For an instant, Alainn felt less threatened by the man, but, as though he thought better of his weakened moment, he leered at her, once more.

"I may no longer need your services as a healer, for I have employed a physician for the castle. He has arrived, only yesterday. He is most esteemed and his practices will surely be more advanced than the remedies you know."

She did not answer.

"You do not appear well pleased with this. Do you truly believe you are as apt at healing as a man who has years of schooling in the area of medicine and surgery?"

"Surgeons can be an asset and I am certain he is well-trained, but will he truly be willing to offer services to all the people in the castle and the village? Or, will he only be interested in healing your clan and your kin?"

"You are a proud woman, Maiden McCreary. There is a haughty mannerism about you that I find quite vain. Not so becoming in a woman." He hissed, "Perhaps, you overestimate your importance here."

" 'Tis a fact I have brought many people much relief and eased the suffering of not a few."

"A learned woman, and one with pride and confidence. The combination is not an affable one, I think. And, you claim to be a seer, as well. Is that why you believe you can assess my sons, because you have second sight?"

"Aye, it assists me at times, in recognizing good and bad in people."

"And how do you see me, Maiden McCreary, as a chieftain, how do you see me?"

"I can hardly answer with candor when you despise me as you seem to, and I doubt I'd care to spend a night in the dungeon because I have wounded your pride."

"No, by all means, enlighten me. How do you see me?"

She was reluctant to begin, but he appeared to be awaiting an answer. "I believe you are mostly a very intelligent and intuitive chieftain. You allow the peasants and servants much say in their own affairs. They are given fair land for their labor. You do not mistreat them, for the most part. Most of your people have ample sustenance and adequate shelter, and they are permitted to barter amongst themselves, even sell their excess for profit. They are able to choose their own wives and decide for themselves regarding personal matters. You do not place strict taxations upon them that force them to steal from you. You maintain their trust, ensuring that, should they need go to battle for you, they will do so willingly and fight for you unfailingly."

"You flatter me, Maiden McCreary. I'd not thought you'd be singing my praises with the disapproving look you have on your face," he sneered.

" 'Tis how you manage your family that most affronts me!" she snapped.

"And, how do you feel I mismanage them?"

"You do not offer them the same regard you give your peasants." His jaw tensed. "You allow them no choices. You decide everything for them, from how they spend their day to who they marry. Their political opinions are to be entirely the same as yours, and you see emotion as a serious flaw. Neither of your sons is ready to take over the chieftainship, but you push them and they both desire to please you so, they will not speak their mind to you for fear they will lose your approval." His brow darkened dangerously. "Instead of concentrating on their strengths, you point out their weaknesses, and you forever compare them to yourself and to each other.

"They are their own persons, both full of great potential

to be sure, but they are vastly different. Your oldest son is a strong warrior. His physical strength is great, his abilities many, but you flay him for not possessing the same aptitude for his studies as your younger son. If he were to take over the chieftainship, any time soon, he would cause widespread devastation, for he would feel the need to conquer all around him." Now that she had started, she could not stop, despite his growing anger. "He would be so eager to show you his power he would ruin all that you have worked to build, and in a matter of months.

"And should you continue to flay your younger son because he is a kind and sensitive man and not as brawny as his brother, he will turn from you. He feels less a man because you assail him when he empathizes with others. That is not a trait to be criticized for a great leader needs some understanding of his men and of the enemies stance. He also possesses great strategic ability. If you allowed them joint-chieftainship, you would remove the competitiveness between them and allow them to focus on what they know, while working still to become more skilled in the areas they do not excel in. If you take away your unreasonable expectations, not rule them so entirely, they would both flourish and grow to be great leaders. And, of matters concerning your wife, you must allow your wife her own beliefs. They are of enormous importance to her!"

"Are you through then, girl?" he exploded. "Have you quite finished with your assessment of my abilities as an earl, a husband, and father?"

"Aye!" she yelled. Her cry echoed through the chamber. Alainn and the chieftain looked at each other, breathing heavily.

"You've not mentioned my nephew. In all your ramblings, you've not included him in our discussion. Surely you have an opinion in how I regard him?"

"You are fair to Killi—" she corrected herself, "to your nephew."

"You do not dwell upon speaking of him, for you know I will detect what fondness you have for him."

She met his gaze evenly. "Aye, I've a fondness for your nephew, as I do for your sons."

"Ah, so you feel the same toward Killian as you do Rory and Riley."

"Not entirely the same, no," she softly added.

"And what do you hope to gain from this closeness you have with my nephew? Do you expect he will relinquish his title, turn his back on his duties, his responsibilities, to take you for his wife?"

"I have no delusions of grandeur, Milord! I have no ulterior motives in caring for Killian. I am in love with him! I will not lie to you, but I have no expectations from what we share."

"I seriously doubt that, Alainn McCreary. There are no women without expectations. Tell me, what exactly do you share with my nephew?" He had moved closer to her and the way he now looked at her left her most uncomfortable. "You know Killian has the potential to become a great chieftain. He has a good head about political matters and the eloquence to sway men to his way of thinking. His alliance with his mother's people is an asset the O'Briens need most assuredly. He is as stubborn as any man I know, and when he wants something, he will move heaven and earth to get it, no matter what the cost."

"But, he is as loyal to you as any man who ever lived."

"Aye, he is loyal, there's no denying that, but if made to choose between loyalty to me or being with you, I am not as confident as I should be in his decision."

"I would never ask him to make that decision, I promise you that! I do not expect him to give up all that he has and will have, for me. That is ludicrous to suggest it! He knows what his path must be. I will never come between what is intended for him."

"I almost believe that," he murmured. "Yet, he has it in his mind it is you he wants, above all else, you he seems willing to fight for."

"That is not what I want!"

"Don't be stupid girl, of course 'tis what you want! If you love him, as you claim to, you surely entertain the romantic fancy that he will sweep you off your feet and carry you away with him where you shall know complete and utter happiness for all time."

"I am not stupid, and I will not allow him to relinquish

his rights, especially not for me."

"And how would you be capable of dissuading him, if that is what he has in mind? You've said yourself, he has a mind of his own."

"He will not turn from all he has ever desired, not for me, not for anyone. He is clear minded, he knows what must be done."

"Aye, most of the time, he does, to be sure, but apparently, as of late, he is ruled by his cock!"

Her eyes narrowed, but she remained silent.

"And is that something you are familiar with as well, Maiden McCreary?" he sneered. "Has my nephew deflowered you, or is he simply the latest in a long list of men who have had you?"

"I am no whore!" she spat.

"But, you allow my nephew to shag you, so you are clearly not virtuous!" She lifted her chin and straightened her shoulders, but did not respond. "You don't deny it, then. You allow him to have you. You give him your honey without objection, without promise of marriage. Then, aye, Alainn McCreary, you are a whore."

Chapter Twenty-Six

H<small>E CAME UP</small> behind her and brushed his body against hers. He placed his hands on her breasts and squeezed hard. She tried to pull away, but he held her tight. "Have you never been forced to partake in such activities?" he whispered into her hair. "Never been used in such a manner by a man?"

She bit her lip to keep silent.

"Clearly you have not," he said, releasing her, "for you are not cowering or shaking. I must conclude you willingly allowed my nephew to take you, but have there been others before him? Do you make it a habit, luring men?" He swept her hair to one side, revealing her long neck. "You are truly beautiful." He brushed it with his hand. "I've never seen the likes of the luster of your hair, or the brilliance of your eyes, the perfection of your skin. And, that lovely scent," he sniffed the air by her ear, "it is captivating. And, your body, well, shall I simply say, I look forward to seeing what lies beneath your frock with great anticipation. What are you, Alainn McCreary?" he said, kissing her neck lightly. She could smell the stale ale on his breath. "What has my nephew so bewitched that he contemplates throwing away everything he has ever wanted for you? Are you a lianhan shee?"

"I am no shee!" she cried, jerking her shoulder to throw him off her. "I am not a love fairy, I do not enslave men, and I wish no ill upon them. I do not tempt men!"

"Ah, but you do!"

"Not intentionally. I have never misled a man or beguiled him!"

"But, you inflict such desire in men they will overcome any obstacle to be with you! My eldest son desires you greatly, I see it in his eyes, and Killian, I fear he is lost, at the moment, for he sees his title and his responsibility toward the O'Briens as nothing but an obstacle in his path to having you. Somehow, you and I must show him you are not worth the trouble or the cost of what he would lose in so doing."

"He will do what is expected of him. He has not spoken of any future plans to me. He knows what we have is only a temporary arrangement, that nothing will come of what we feel for one another," she said desperately.

"He has not spoken of any of his intentions toward you?"

"No, he has not! I have told him on more than one occasion that I know he will be wed to another, that, one day, he will return to his father's castle and rule his lands."

"Aye, and I have found the perfect match for him. He was not entirely overjoyed with the notion, but I assume he will come to his senses when he sees her. He goes now, even as we speak, to retrieve her." Alainn gasped. The chieftain smiled wickedly. "I have heard she is quite a lovely young maiden. A Scot, now living with her aunt and uncle. She is a cousin to the sisters McDonnel who will wed my sons. Her father is the great Scottish Chieftain, Ian MacDonald. Their marriage would ensure a strong allegiance of the clans and a stronghold against the English if we are made to fight them."

He had stepped back from her and his expression was thoughtful, no longer distorted with lust. Alainn felt as if her heart were being squeezed. Killian would bring back his future wife. Nothing would ever be the same between them.

"You seem somewhat distracted Maiden McCreary. Does it displease you greatly to know he will soon share his life and his bed with another woman, a woman who is his equal, not a lowly servant? I suspect it will take some convincing on both our parts for him to go through with the intended marriage, but we will accomplish it, won't we Alainn McCreary?"

She felt her hot tears close to the surface, but she took a deep breath and spoke. "He will marry her. I will see to it."

"Aye, but we must make her seem incredibly appealing and you less than perfect as he sees you now. How might we accomplish that, do you suppose?" He sat on the edge of the table in front of her. "I have thought on little else these last few days. I have come up with a few plans that might be successful. None, I'm sure, you'd find terribly appealing."

"I will simply tell him we are through. Whatever has

passed between us is over. He will not pursue our relationship, not if I discourage it."

"Ah, perhaps, I was hasty in assuming you are haughty and proud, for I fear you do not give yourself enough credit. He burns for you," he crooned. "He can see no one or nothing when it comes to you. Christ, he is considering giving up everything that was once important to him, just to ensure he has you. He'll not give up his intent toward you without a formidable fight. And, by that time, the young Maiden MacDonald and her uncle may not find him and his chieftainship so appealing. Something more drastic must be undertaken. I had thought to have you killed." He smiled at the thought. "Truly, thrown in the peat bog. Or, sent away on a slave ship to the Americas, for they have begun a most lucrative business in such commodities. But, I am certain my nephew would search for you, perhaps go to the ends of the earth to find out why you left him without word. So, I fear that course of action will not do."

"You need not kill me, I assure you," she said, tears welling in her eyes. "I can make him see reason. He will listen to me."

"Even so, he will still desire you and you him. So, we must take away your desires toward one another. Perhaps, if you were unappealing to him, or if you were no longer willing to be with him in a physical manner, that might accomplish it. That does affect the way a man desires a woman, when she no longer has physical desires."

"Your wife still has desires."

He looked into her eyes, his displeasure and his pain evident. "What do you know of my wife's desires?"

"I know she cares enough for you not to turn to another man to sate her passion. Instead, she takes a remedy to calm all desire. I know she still yearns to be with you, but will not risk another lost child."

"And, do you know of these things because of your position as herbalist or healer, or because you are a seer?"

"Some of the secrets I am privy to are due to my knowledge of herbs and who seeks their assistance for ails and ills, but, aye, some I know by way of my visions."

"And, what secrets do you possess that would be of interest to me?"

"I suspect there are few things in the castle or the village that are kept secret from you, else, you would not know what Killian and I share."

"One only has to look at Killian to know he burns for you," he scoffed, "and it doesn't take a seer to know in the past weeks he has been absent from the castle as much as he's been here, and by his unquestionable good mood of late, I suspected he was dipping his wick. Though, I'd not known who the girl might be that was accommodating him." He placed his hands on her hips. "For a time, I thought perhaps he had renewed his relationship with the miller's daughter, or the cobbler's pretty little daughter, maybe the tailor's lass, or perhaps half a dozen others he's had through the years.

But, it was a servant I employed to keep watch on him that told me it was you who he spends his nights with, you who his cock throbs for this time." His hands squeezed her tightly.

Alainn tried to keep her growing jealousy off her face.

"You are not so pleased to hear about the women who have shared such activities with my nephew. How do you suppose you will deal with the knowledge he takes a wife, a beautiful young Scottish lass who will share his bed whenever he requires?"

"It will be of little consequence to me when they have wed, for they will be far from here."

"And, if they stayed here for a time, after their marriage? Would you become his mistress?"

"I would not!"

"So you say, but I am reluctant to believe you can turn away from him so easily, if you have the feelings for him that you claim to have. But," he said, kneading her hips slightly. "You have yet to tell me what secrets you know. Perhaps, you are truly no seer, at all and only pretend to know things."

"How would I benefit from that? I have never tried to use my visions to better myself."

"Then, tell me what secrets you know of my kin to begin with," he said impatiently. "Tell me what you know regarding my brother, Sean."

"I know his wife was not of noble birth, that she was a

commoner. I know she died in childbed."

"Aye, you are partly correct. She was a commoner, and she did die shortly after giving birth to her son. But, you see no other secret surrounding her and my brother?"

"If you are inquiring to find if I know the child is not your brother's son, aye, I am aware of it. I know she could not conceive a child. She sought another man, became with child and bore a son."

"And, do you know the paternity of the boy?"

"Aye, I do. Do you?"

"I do as well, but tell me so that I might have further faith in your abilities."

"Or you might punish the father?"

"You are as suspicious of me as I am of you, I think," he said admiringly.

"I am mostly curious as to why you would allow the boy to be raised an O'Brien, and that you permit your brother to think of him as his son."

"The boy should not be made to pay for his mother's indiscretions, and, I suppose, it was to give the rest of my line hope that a child might be a possibility. The woman was made to pay for her deception, and my brother grieved for her most terribly. It would have been cruel to take both of them away from him."

"You caused her death? She did not die in childbed?"

"You didn't see that with your powers? Though in all fairness, I suppose, you would have only been a child when the deed was done. The midwife was instructed to give the woman a dose of cowbane."

"Which in small amounts can be used to dull pain, but in a large quantity it is a most effective poison."

"Aye, so it won't be so easy to get rid of you in that manner, since you are of a suspicious nature and have exceedingly good knowledge of herbs. I suppose poisoning will not be an option."

"You have no need to dispose of me. I have told you so and I am good as my word."

The chieftain moved away from her to refill his goblet. His eyes were becoming more glazed, and she hoped soon he would simply pass out in a drunken stupor. He caught her eyeing the goblet.

"Do you have some potions, some magic ingredient you plan to spike my drink with?"

"I would hardly cause you harm when to do so would be to sign my own death warrant."

"Otherwise you might be so inclined?" he queried.

"I have no intention of causing you harm."

"Even knowing I am contemplating causing you great harm, and knowing I caused the death of my sister-in-law."

"I am less than pleased by the news, for I thought you were an honorable man."

"If a neighboring clan had plans to attack my castle and kill my clan and kin, and I caught wind of it, would I not be wise to attack them first?"

"Aye, I believe you would have little choice to protect what is yours."

"This is no different, Alainn McCreary. I am protecting what is mine.

"If Sean had learned his wife was unfaithful to him, he would have felt entirely betrayed, as it is, he grieves for the woman he loved, but her memory is not tarnished. My dealing with you will surely be to the same end. Killian will lose his title and all he holds dear to be with a woman that would not be worthy of his love, for, surely, you would hurt him in the same adulterous manner."

"I would never hurt him, and I assure you I would not be unfaithful to him! Why do you believe it would be so? Because, I am of common birth? Are you naïve enough to believe only women of lowly birth can be unfaithful?"

"I actually meant beautiful women, in general," he raked his eyes over her. "When enough attention is paid to them by men, they almost always give in to their desires, and I would imagine there will be many men who want you. And, to that end, I had thought perhaps to have a dozen or so of my guards take you to some far-off forest and have their way with you for as long and as in as vicious a manner as necessary to ensure you never feel anything but repulsion or loathing at the thought of a man even touching you, ever again."

"And, you could find that many dishonorable men within your guard?"

"I could find that many men who would obey my orders no matter what those orders might be. Don't fool yourself, girl!"

"You sent the steward's sons after me, didn't you? It was not on their own accord that they followed us."

"Aye, but the captain's son seems intent on keeping close tabs on you. I thought the two objectionable men would be capable of tormenting you enough to accomplish the deed of making you frigid, as they seem most unscrupulous. I thought to save my guards any uneasiness in doing what they may later regret, especially since most of them have a deep respect for Killian."

"How very thoughtful of you, 'tis a pity you don't have the same regard or respect for Killian."

"I do what I must, girl. I can hardly lose sleep over what is done for the good of the O'Briens."

"But, your cohorts were a bit lacking in the ability to overtake Pierce, and the younger no match for my dagger."

"Aye, I was informed of their bungling the task. I had not counted on Killian providing a guard for you in his stead. And, in regards to the dagger you possess, I would request you hand it over to me, at once."

She stepped back, holding the dagger possessively in her pocket. "I always keep it close at hand to fight off any who attempt misdeeds toward me."

"And, I suppose there have been many?"

"Enough to warrant keeping it close."

"Which is exactly why I would have you give it to me, now. While I am sure you are aware an attempt on my life would be an offense punishable by death, I will not risk losing any vital parts."

"What do you plan to do to me?"

"Use your powers of sight woman! What do you suppose I intend to do to you? I intend to find out for myself what it is to be with a woman who evokes such desire that a man is willing to toss aside everything else that is important to him."

He lunged toward her and grabbed her. He pulled her into his body, his hot breath on her neck. Reaching into her pocket, he retrieved the dagger and flung it across the room. Then, he pulled her hair away from her neck, his rough kisses bruising her skin. She pushed away from him but he caught her arm and yanked her back to him, forcing his lips on hers. She bit his lip and he laughed.

"I am not adverse to a wee bit of fighting, girl. In truth, it often proves to cause added excitement." He ground his pelvis against her. "Just don't wound me too severely on my face. The celebrations are soon to be held, and the scratches might be a bit difficult to explain."

Chapter Twenty-Seven

H E THREW HER down onto the table and her head hit it hard. His hands were on her dress and she heard the garment rip. He tore away the chemise underneath. She screamed, and he slapped her hard across the face.

"What purpose will raping me serve?" she cried.

"I expect it will be most enjoyable, and my nephew will not be able to think of you as only his any longer."

"But, he will hate you for this!"

"Perhaps, for a time, but I assure you, he will no longer think of you in the same way, either. And, how could he be entirely sure it was rape? He will surely have doubts as to whether you felt compelled to offer your chieftain a bit of your honey, as well."

Her dress was torn from neck to waist and her breasts, exposed. She tried to cover herself, but he grabbed both her arms and held them high above her head with force. She could feel her wrists bruising and her shoulders aching. With his other hand, he attempted to lift her skirts. She kicked at him, lifted her knees and tried to connect with his privates. His hands bruised the soft flesh on her inner thighs and she felt hot tears rolling down her cheeks. With his knee, he forced her legs apart and positioned himself between her thighs. He worked at the fastenings on his trews. His hand grabbed the part of her previously only touched by Killian, and she screamed in outrage, tried to buck him off. This only proved to spur him on.

She closed her eyes and felt herself growing dizzy. The table began to shake. The jug crashed to the ground. The man barely seemed to notice.

"Your sons will lose complete respect of you for this!" she screamed.

"How would they know it was not you who tempted me? You are allowing their cousin to have his way with you whenever and wherever he desires it! Do you think they would believe you wouldn't offer yourself to me? I am the earl!"

"Think of your wife!"

"She refuses to share my bed, so to hell with her! She has brought this on as much as you!"

"He will kill you for this!" she cried. "Killian will run you through for this!"

"Kill his uncle? Assassinate the chieftain? He is not above the law! He would hang for the deed no matter what prompted it!" The man was panting from the effort of fighting her. His trews were now down to his knees, his lust, evident. Her skirts were pushed up to her waist and he would soon accomplish what he'd set out to do.

She looked at the goblet on the table and sent it flying toward the man. He ducked, glaring at her with a mixture of horror and fascination, but was not deterred. She stared at the animal heads on the walls and imaged their sounds in life. Soon, roaring and snorting filled the room and, this time, the chieftain's face grew pale. She set the table to shaking again and the many sets of antlers above fell from their mounts. The statue of the man on the horse at the far end of the room came crashing down and broke into hundreds of pieces. The fire roared wildly and the blaze licked the enormous ceiling.

The chieftain hesitated and she kicked him hard, sending him sprawling backwards. She tried to roll off the table, but he was back at her before she could put her feet to the ground. He threw her down on the table, her face smacked the surface, as he hiked up her skirts. He grabbed her throat and squeezed so hard, she thought he might strangle her. Tears poured down her cheeks. When she spotted her dagger on the floor across the room, she willed it to come to her and when he heard it whistling across the room, he jumped back. She lunged for him and caught his hand with the tip. He cried out but charged at her again. She held the blade out in front of her and started to move from the table. He found his sword, unsheathed it, and held it out toward her throat, holding her in place.

"What are you? Are you a witch? Is that what allows you to call objects to you?"

She was shaking so hard she could not speak. Tears poured from her eyes, blurring her sight, and in perfect clarity she saw a vision. It was the Glade Witch, her mother, Mara, and she was being violated by a man, Hugh O'Brien's father. Here on this very table, in this very room. She could hear her begging for him to stop, but he raped her and beat her and even when she told him of the child she carried, he would not relent. Alainn could hear her cries, her painful screams. She saw the objects moving in the room, just as they had been, moments ago.

Alainn slowly backed away from the sword, her eyes blazing with fury. Seeing the injustices done to her mother, she understood what had caused her to curse the O'Brien. Alainn heard the words within her head. But, she did not speak them. She tried to think of a spell that would affect only this man, but she could not find an appropriate curse. Killian was still too important to her. She could not do harm to this man. Not yet.

She backed up toward the door and looked at the man. Assessing his body, she found his weakness. An old injury to his leg, a break, she suspected. She dwelled upon that part and watched his face twist in pain. She continued backing up while the man screamed out in terror and anguish. She was halfway to the door, when the priest came down the back stairs and entered the great hall, looking with concern at the screaming man.

She hid her weapon deep within her pocket and tried to

cover herself with her torn garments. The priest went to the chieftain's side, not in the least disturbed by the fact his trews were now down to his ankles. She released the man's pain and he hastened to clothe himself.

"What has she done to you, Milord?"

"What have I done to him?" she hissed. Her throat hurt terribly and her voice came out in a raspy whisper. "Can you not see what has happened, what he has attempted to do to me?" The priest ignored her completely.

"Should I have the guards seize her? Should she be thrown in the dungeon?"

The chieftain looked fearfully at Alainn and hesitated. "No, Father, let her go. For now, let her be. But, when my nephew arrives home, you may tell him what you've seen. She was nearly naked, you'll recall, and, it was obvious what we had been doing. And, if you want to exaggerate the telling somewhat, suggest it was her who initiated the entire event. I'd be much obliged to you."

Hugh O'Brien stared at her with a look that would curdle blood, and she looked back with equal loathing. "How could I have been so wrong about a man?" she rasped, holding her throat. "I truly believed you were honorable."

"Keep your nose clean, girl," he snapped. "Go about your duties, as you always have, and you may keep the room in the castle, for a time. But, you will not spend time with my nephew again. Do or say whatever is necessary to ensure he has no hope the two of you will ever have a future together. And, to ensure he forgets about you and concentrates his efforts on the woman who is to be his wife, we will find you a husband. Think on that for a time. Father, do you know of men seeking a wife at this time? Sometimes, they come to you for assistance in that area."

"Aye, there are some to be sure. The swine handler has shown some interest in taking a wife," he said with a sneer.

"Ah, wouldn't that be an ironic turn of events if the man who slops the hogs was to wed the lovely, educated Maiden McCreary? I'm sure they could make a happy home in the hovel next to the hog pens."

Alainn knew of the man. He was, by no fault of his own a filthy sort. He probably never washed and always reeked of the hogs he tended. His face and hair had surely not seen water in years. She considered what it would be to be wed to him and reasoned, if the chieftain and the priest decided it would be so, she could find herself wed to him this very day. She swallowed hard.

"The widower McLean has expressed a need for a new wife. His wife has been gone for nearly a year now," the priest added.

The widower McLean was past six decades with a foul smell that permeated from him, as well. His was the odor of unwashed elderly man, and the thought of sharing his home, much less his bed, made her stomach turn.

"I have heard the farmer, O'Hara, is in need of a wife," the chieftain said, his tone softening somewhat. "His wife died in childbed last winter. He has a child to care for. He is a good man, I believe, with an ample home and many sheep. He would surely be capable of providing for a wife and many more children."

He was giving her a way out, a reasonable escape and a way to lead a normal life. He was suggesting if she married this man, left Killian to the wife he had planned for him, he would forget what had transpired in this room today, and allow her to live, even knowing what capabilities she possessed.

Liam O'Hara was a kind man, a gentle and loving man. She'd been called to assist the midwife when his child had been born, as was the case on occasion. She'd been present when the man had seen his son for the first time. She'd witnessed firsthand his pride, the complete joy on his face when he held his son. And, when his wife faded due to complications during the birth, she'd seen the pain in his gentle blue eyes. He'd wept unabashedly and then held her to him after the woman had passed. He was a pleasant-looking man, as well, and his home and garden were lovely. "I will be in close contact with you, Maiden McCreary, and when the celebrations for my sons have ended, we will discuss this further. Until then, I will expect you to bend to my will for there is still the matter of a horse that went missing from my stables, yesterday. That, we have yet to discuss. And, when my nephew returns you know what must be done. If he is not convinced it is in everyone's best interest for him to marry the Scottish lass, it could be perceived as a slight to me. Perhaps, even treasonous in nature, if he won't marry for the good of our clan. And, we both know what punishment is issued for treason."

"You would not see him harmed?" she asked, her disbelief clear on her face. "Do not harm him, Hugh O'Brien!" she begged.

"I will do what I must!"

Pointing her finger at him, she warned, "If peril should befall him by your hand or your order, you will be made to suffer."

"You dare to threaten me, girl?"

"Aye. If you hurt him in any way, I swear to you the curse Mara uttered will seem mildly irritating to what I will conjure for you and your priest. That is a promise, and I believe you know I am capable of accomplishing much."

She glanced up at the one set of antlers remaining on the wall, the treasured giant Irish elk horns, and concentrated a moment. They shook, fell, and shattered, not far from where the two men stood. With that, Alainn turned and fled the room, her back to the chieftain. She went up the back stairs towards her bedchamber, but only made it halfway up the narrow steps before she sunk to the ground and wept, her body shaking uncontrollably.

The bruises on her wrists and throat ached, and she could see dark impressions of his fingers where he had pinched and prodded her tender swollen breasts. She would never speak of this to Killian, she could never speak of this to anyone. Her stomach responded to the ordeal and she wretched violently, spewing the contents of her stomach on the steps.

Chapter Twenty-Eight

ALAINN CLOSED HER eyes and pulled the cloak more tightly over her head, hoping to prevent the bitter wind and persistent drizzle from chilling her further. The day's weather reflected her dismal mood most assuredly, and the constant bumps and thumps of the cart's wheels beneath her worsened her already queasy stomach. She had clearly not been thinking when she embarked upon this impulsive journey. When she had spotted Cookson readying the cart for his ride to Galway for supplies, she had simply envisioned an escape.

The previous day, the chieftain had a servant follow her everywhere she went, and Pierce remained intent on watching over her every move. Though she had yearned to speak with Mara or Morag, again, she could not attempt a visit with the Glade Witch or conjure Morag's recently departed spirit with so many eyes upon her.

Inside the castle walls, this very morning, she had dared to stand near the top of the winding steps leading to the dungeon in hope of using her powers to detect the hidden portion of the amulet. But, she could sense nothing. Her stomach remained putrid and her body still revealed many bruises and tender spots. Her lingering despair felt like it might consume her.

Killian would surely be back to Castle O'Brien by nightfall, and Alainn felt she could not bear to see him arrive with the woman who was to be his wife. She longed to have him take her in his arms and proclaim his love, once again, but she recalled the chieftain's threatening words. She would not put Killian in danger.

Alainn had briefly considered marrying the farmer O'Hara. Perhaps, that would be the easiest path for her. Yet, she doubted she could look upon Killian's face when she related her intentions of marrying another. Her head grew so muddled and her heart so filled with melancholia, that the weather had responded. The cold drizzle had set in and the bitter wind had begun.

It made the graveside ceremony for Morag most unpleasant but understandably short. Alainn's warm tears had slid down her cheeks as the cold rain soaked through her garments to her skin. The chieftain had said a few hurried words before taking leave to seek shelter. Lady Siobhan had hugged her tightly and kissed her cheek before accompanying her husband. Molly had held tight to Alainn's hand, and Cook and Margaret, along with their entire family and most of the kitchen servants, had lingered to pay tribute to the old healer. Although Alainn would have remained, Cook had gently led her back to the kitchen where he fixed her a warm broth. They had eaten silently by the hearth's warm fire, Molly at her side the entire time, hoping to ease Alainn's grief and loneliness.

Cook had not yet found a private moment to speak with her regarding her audience with the chieftain. Alainn was most relieved. She knew it would be difficult to hide her emotions from this kind man who had acted as her father for a good portion of her life. No good would come of Cook avenging the wrongdoings done to her at the chieftain's hands. In truth, Cook and his entire family could be made to suffer simply by affiliating with Alainn. Twice more, Alainn had seen the priest and, both times, he had glared with such loathing, she had turned away from his cold eyes. She had wanted to harm the horrid man and had to suppress envisioning his torture. The power hummed in her veins as though it fought to be released and she had sensed a dizziness overtaking her. She feared that her powers had become restless and unpredictable, that she was no longer able to control her abilities and might harm the priest or the chieftain. She knew she must leave this place. Sure, there was nothing more to hold her at Castle O'Brien.

Alainn had briefly considered going to the fairy glade. But, without her amulet to ensure safe passage within, she dared not attempt it. And, to be certain, the Unseelie Court would sense her despairing heart and fearful spirit, and latch onto her. She knew she must depart from the castle, the chieftain, his priest, and all the misery that surrounded her.

Although fleeing this place would not free her from unpleasantness, it might buy her some time, and, perhaps, once away, she could think of a way to end or at the very least to weaken the curse.

When Cookson had secured the cart and sat upon the wagon's seat, he had smiled and waved at Alainn, given command to the two horses, and set off. The guard the chieftain had employed to watch over her had stepped within a doorway, attempting to warm himself. Pierce was across the pathway, also preoccupied with the miserable weather. Alainn had watched as Cookson neared the drawbridge, then she began to run, a basket of herbs cradled in her arm.

She reached the cart and unceremoniously threw herself onto the back of the cart, landing upon the many tarps that lay within. Although she had called upon the wind to heighten, in the hope of distracting Cookson and the horses, they had turned to find they had acquired another passenger. Cookson slowed and stopped the horses, just as a breathless and obviously irritated Pierce caught up to them.

Both young men held similar displeased expressions. Pierce gasped for breath, unable to form words.

"What are you about, Alainn?" demanded Cookson. "What are you doin'?"

"Leaving Castle O'Brien. Going to Galway."

"You cannot!" both men shouted.

"Aye, I can, and I will," she insisted, her jaw set, her face determined. "There is nothing to hold me to this place any longer."

"What of your duties as a healer?" Cookson asked in disbelief.

"The chieftain has hired a surgeon. My services as healer to the O'Briens are no longer needed."

"But, what of Killian? He has asked me to watch over you. What of your... your love for each other?" Pierce stammered.

"Killian is off fetching his intended," Alainn said miserably. "They shall be wedded, soon." She fought valiantly to control her composure. "And the chieftain is set to marry me off, perhaps, to the swine handler or the widower MacLean." Alainn's voice caught on the sob she could no longer stifle.

The two young men exchanged a look of revulsion at the suggestion and Pierce clambered up on to the seat beside Cookson.

"What are you doing, Pierce?" Alainn asked, now crying in earnest.

"Seeing you safe to Galway," he said firmly.

"But your father—"

"I am a grown man and my father will know my reasoning when it is explained to him." Pierce's firm tone was steeped in finality.

Alainn was too cold, tired, and disheartened to argue further, even knowing the captain of the guard would surely be made to fret regarding his son's whereabouts.

The guard at the drawbridge paid little attention to the

three travelers as he signaled for the bridge to be lifted. Alainn settled in her position in the cart, her mind returning to the previous thought. Would she ever return to Castle O'Brien? Her powers of perception, never clear when attempting to see her own destiny, seemed to elude her entirely. She huddled behind a large keg and pulled the cloak over her face.

In time, all would be revealed. She placed a hand to her swelling belly and was almost certain she felt a tiny movement beneath it. Surely it was too soon. She closed her eyes and attempted to harden her heart to what the future may bring to her and all that she held dear. Aye, surely, time would hold the answer of what fate held in store for the witch's daughter.

THE END

If you enjoyed The Farrier's Daughter, make sure to check out the rest of Leigh Ann Edwards' newest series!

THE IRISH WITCH SERIES

Book One: The Farrier's Daughter

Book Two: The Witch's Daughter

Book Three: The Chieftain's Daughter

ABOUT THE AUTHOR

Since she was a child, Leigh Ann Edwards has always had a vivid imagination and lots of stories to tell. An enthusiastic traveler and author for over twenty years, her adventures in Massachusetts, Ireland, and the UK inspired The Farrier's Daughter and its sequel novels in the Irish Witch series. Edwards adores animals, history, genealogy, and magical places—and Ireland is filled with many magical places. She lives with her husband and two cats in the lovely city of Edmonton, Alberta.

Visit Leigh Ann at www.leighannedwards.com

Thank you for reading

The Farrier's Daughter

If you enjoyed this book, you can find more from all our great authors at TulePublishing.com, or from your favorite online retailer.

TULE
PUBLISHING

Made in the USA
San Bernardino, CA
24 February 2018